TRAIL OF HOPE

Copyright © 2024 by Jason F. Anderson

All rights reserved.

No part of this publication may be reproduced, distributed, or transmitted in any form or by any means, including photocopying, recording, or other electronic or mechanical methods, without the publisher's prior written permission, except as permitted by U.S. copyright law.

The story, all names, characters, and incidents portrayed in this production are fictitious. No identification with actual persons (living or deceased), places, buildings, and products is intended or should be inferred.

Prologue

In the spring of 1843, nearly a thousand settlers gathered in Independence, Missouri, their wagons laden with dreams of Oregon's promised valleys. They came from all walks of life—farmers, carpenters, merchants, and artisans—each carrying generations of Eastern skills toward an uncertain Western future. This great migration would mark the first major wagon train to traverse the Oregon Trail, blazing a path that countless others would follow.

The journey stretched roughly two thousand miles across half a continent. Those who attempted it faced a gauntlet of natural obstacles: the muddy Missouri plains, the harsh Platte River Valley, the towering Rocky Mountains, and the scorching Snake River desert. Disease, accidents, and the unforgiving elements claimed many lives along the way. Yet still they came, drawn by stories of fertile soil and fresh beginnings in Oregon's Willamette Valley.

For these pioneers, leaving meant abandoning more than just their homes. They left behind family networks, established trades, and the certainty of familiar seasons. They traded comfort for courage and security for possibility. Many sold their possessions for wagon space, keeping only what tools and treasures might serve them in their new lives.

The trail demanded everything they could give—strength, determination, and unwavering faith in what lay ahead. But it gave strange gifts in return: children who grew capable beyond their years, women who found reserves of untapped courage, and men who learned that true craft could survive any journey. Some families grew stronger through loss, while others discovered that survival sometimes meant learning new ways to read old signs.

This is the story of one such family—the Wheelers of Pennsylvania—who carried five generations of craft and tradition toward Oregon's distant shore. Their journey would test their physical endurance and understanding of what makes a home. Like many others who attempted the trail that year, they would learn that some treasures can only be found by leaving everything familiar behind.

The Great Emigration of 1843 began America's westward expansion in earnest. But beyond the historical significance lies a more intimate truth: sometimes, the most extraordinary journeys are measured not in miles traveled but in how far the heart can grow while crossing unknown territory.

1

THE CARPENTER'S DREAM

Pennsylvania, January 1843

As Caleb Wheeler descended to his workshop in the predawn darkness, the wooden stairs creaked with each careful step. His right leg, stiff from the night's chill, forced a slight hesitation between steps. The scent of pine shavings and linseed oil greeted him as he stepped off the bottom step. Reaching through the darkness, he was able to find the lamp. Striking a match against the workbench, he saw rows of old tools hanging on the wall.

As he moved through the workshop, he set out the tools he would need for the current project. His fingers traced the edge of a partially completed dovetail joint, testing its precision. The oak would need another day of curing before completing the join. Harrison's daughter's wedding wasn't for another three weeks—time enough if the banker didn't change the terms again.

The first hint of dawn crept through the workshop's eastern window, casting a faint light across the sawdust-strewn floor. Caleb's leg protested as he bent to retrieve a fallen plane, the old injury from a scaffolding accident nearly ending his career a decade ago. The sound of footsteps overhead told him Sarah was awake, and soon, the rich aroma of coffee drifted down the stairs.

"You're up early," Sarah said, appearing at the workshop door with two steaming cups. Her brown hair was already neatly braided, though wisps had escaped around her face. She handed him a cup, the routine so familiar neither spoke as he took his first sip.

Sarah reached up to straighten his collar, her fingers lingering momentarily. "The Mitchells canceled their appointment. Third one this week."

Before Caleb could respond, the sharp crack of wood on wood echoed through the workshop. Thomas burst through the door, wielding a wooden sword with all the fury his seven years could muster.

"Take that, wild Indian!" Thomas shouted, jabbing at imaginary foes. His brown hair was stuck in untamed cowlicks, and his nightshirt was still untucked.

"Thomas Wheeler," Sarah called, "if you don't get dressed properly for breakfast, the only thing you'll be fighting is an empty stomach."

The boy retreated, his wooden sword trailing behind him. Caleb watched him go, noting the frayed edges of his nightshirt. New clothes would have to wait, like many other things.

"Harrison's coming about the chest today," Caleb said, his voice low. "Said he needs to discuss the terms."

Sarah raised an eyebrow in concern. "He can't change the price again. We've already bought the oak."

"Times are hard for everyone," Caleb replied, though the words tasted bitter. He returned to his workbench, not wanting Sarah to see the worry in his eyes. The ledger on the wall, its pages increasingly empty, seemed to mock him from its nail.

The workshop door burst open again, admitting Jimmy Patterson, the newspaper boy. His face was red from running, and the latest edition of the Williamsport Gazette was clutched in his hand.

"Mr. Wheeler! You won't believe the news from Oregon!" Jimmy thrust the paper forward. "They say a man can claim three hundred and twenty acres just for settling there!"

Caleb exchanged a glance with Sarah before fishing in his pocket for payment. Finding only wood shavings and a miniature carved horse he'd made the day before, he held out the toy. "Will this do for today, Jimmy?"

The boy's eyes lit up as he grabbed the wooden horse, nearly dropping the paper in his haste. "Sure will, Mr.

Wheeler! Ma says your carvings are worth more than money anyway."

As Jimmy darted away, Emma appeared in the doorway, Caleb's forgotten lunch pail in her hands. At ten, she showed signs of Sarah's grace in her movements, though her green eyes were all his.

"You forgot this, Pa," she said, setting the pail on his workbench. Her gaze drifted to the newspaper Jimmy had left, lingering on the headlines about Oregon.

Caleb unfolded the newspaper, his coffee cooling forgotten beside him. The front page spoke of fertile valleys, timber-rich mountains, and land free for the taking. His fingers traced the words as he read, sawdust falling from his hands onto the ink.

Emma lingered by the workbench as Caleb set aside the newspaper. He picked up a piece of scrap oak and his marking knife, gesturing for her to come closer.

"Watch carefully now," he said, positioning her hands on the wood. Dovetails need a steady hand and a patient eye." He took her hand and showed her how to mark the angle. Emma's concentration showed in the slight wrinkle of her brow, the same expression Sarah wore when measuring herbs for her midwifery.

Again, the workshop door swung open as Thomas ran in, now adequately dressed but still holding his wooden sword. "The Indians are attacking the fort!" he shouted as he ducked behind a table. "Quick, Emma! Help defend the walls!"

"Thomas Wheeler," Caleb said, his voice stern but unable to hide a smile, "if you knock over that pine I spent two days curing, you'll be defending yourself from more than Indians."

Little Margaret followed after her brother, her new cornhusk doll clutched tight in one hand. Her blonde curls, different from her siblings' darker hair, bounced with each step. She approached the large pile of sawdust in the corner and began to make footprints.

"Margaret, no!" Sarah's warning came from the top of the stairs. "Caleb, don't let her near that sawdust pile. Last time, she was sneezing for days."

Caleb scooped up his youngest before she could reach her goal, ignoring the protest from his leg as he lifted her. Margaret giggled and reached for his beard with her free hand, the doll swinging precariously from the other.

"Pa," Emma said, still focused on the dovetail marking, "why does Mr. Harrison need such a fancy chest for his daughter? Seems awful expensive in times like these."

The innocent question struck harder than she could know. Caleb set Margaret down carefully and turned to the delivery ledger on the wall. Once filled with orders months in advance, its pages showed more crossed-out entries than active ones.

"Some folks still believe appearances matter more than sense," he answered finally, running his finger down the latest cancellations page. The Morris family's cradle, the church's new pew ends, the Blacksmith's storage chest – all canceled or "postponed indefinitely."

A sharp knock at the workshop door interrupted his thoughts. Caleb saw Harrison's well-maintained coat and polished boots through the window. The banker's daughter's wedding chest sat unfinished on the workbench, only half-complete.

"Emma, take your sister upstairs," Caleb said quietly, straightening his work apron. "Thomas, your mother could use help with the morning chores."

Emma gathered Margaret quickly, understanding in her eyes too old for her years. Thomas opened his mouth to protest but caught his sister's warning look and followed, wooden sword dragging behind him.

Harrison didn't wait for an invitation before stepping inside. He removed his hat, revealing carefully oiled hair, and cleared his throat.

"Wheeler," he said. "About my Katherine's chest. Given the current economic conditions, I've had to reassess my expenditures." He paused as he glanced at the half-finished piece. "I'm afraid I can only offer half the agreed price."

Caleb's hands tightened on his work apron, knuckles whitening. The oak for the chest cost a month's earnings and was ordered specially from the lumber mill two towns over. Even at the original price, his profit would have been thin.

"Mr. Harrison," he began, keeping his voice level, "the wood alone-"

"Is already cut and partially worked, yes," Harrison interrupted. "Which is why I'm offering anything at all. Times are difficult for everyone, Wheeler. Surely you understand that."

Movement by the stairs caught Caleb's eye. Emma stood in the shadows, one hand pressed against her mouth, watching. She shouldn't have to see this, he thought. She shouldn't have to understand such things at her age.

Sarah appeared suddenly at the workshop door, Margaret on her hip. "Mr. Harrison, pardon the interruption, but Caleb is needed urgently. Mrs. Thompson's baby furniture requires immediate attention." The lie fell smoothly from her lips, her face composed despite the flash of anger in her eyes.

Harrison replaced his hat, offering Sarah a slight bow. "Of course, Mrs. Wheeler. We can discuss terms another time." He turned back to Caleb. "Though I should mention, the Petersons over in Millvale are offering very reasonable rates for custom work these days."

After Harrison left, Caleb stood silently, staring at the unfinished chest. Sarah set Margaret down and came to stand beside him, her hand finding his.

"We'll manage," she said softly. "We always have."

But Caleb's eyes had drifted to the newspaper on his workbench, its headlines about Oregon still visible beneath the sawdust.

When the workshop emptied, Caleb pulled his ledger from its nail and sat heavily at his workbench. The account books told a story more evident than any newspaper – column after column of crossed-out orders and adjusted prices. He traced each entry with his finger, remembering the promises those orders had held months ago.

The letter from his cousin Timothy in Missouri lay hidden beneath the ledger's back cover. He withdrew it now, the paper already worn at the creases from repeated reading. Timothy's words spoke of opportunity: wagon trains gathering, families joining together, three hundred and twenty acres free for the claiming. The next train would leave Independence in early spring.

Caleb's eyes fell on his grandfather's tools, arranged precisely on the wall. Five generations of Wheelers had worked wood in Pennsylvania, and their reputation was built through decades of honest craft. The planer had been his grandfather's wedding gift, and its handle was smooth from years of use—the thought of selling such tools twisted in his gut like a bent nail.

Sarah's soft step on the workshop stairs barely registered until she spoke. "She's finally asleep," she said, gesturing upstairs, where Margaret napped in a pile of fresh wood shavings, her favorite spot despite Sarah's protests. "I found her trying to build a fort with your oak scraps."

Caleb quickly folded Timothy's letter, but not before Sarah saw it. Her eyes lingered on the Missouri postmark before shifting to the ledger spread before him.

"How bad?" she asked.

"Harrison's not the only one looking to halve his prices," Caleb replied, turning the ledger so she could see. "The Mills family canceled their order entirely. They said they're leaving for Indiana and looking for better prospects."

"Indiana," Sarah repeated softly. "Seems everyone's looking west these days."

A knock interrupted them. Reverend Mills stood in the doorway. The man's eyes showed signs of fatigue and worry.

"Brother Wheeler," he said, stepping inside. "About the church pews..."

"The repair can wait, Reverend," Caleb started, but Mills raised a hand.

"That's not why I'm here." He moved closer, lowering his voice. "Word came from the Petersons. They've reached Oregon safely. Good land, they say. Fertile soil, timber aplenty." He paused, glancing at Sarah, who pretended to be busy with sweeping. "They say a man with skills like yours could build a fine life there."

Emma's shadow moved behind the lumber stack, and Caleb knew she was listening. Thomas crouched in the flower bed outside the workshop windows, practicing "scouting." The boy's fascination with frontier life had only grown since the Oregon stories began circulating.

"Five families from the congregation have already committed to the spring wagons," Mills continued. "Good families, skilled people. The kind of community that could take root and grow."

Caleb's leg throbbed as if reminding him of its weakness. "The journey's long, Reverend. Dangerous."

"Life's dangerous here too, in its way," Mills replied, his eyes moving to the empty ledger. "The Petersons mentioned your cousin Timothy's been helping organize the trains."

Sarah's sweeping had stopped entirely, though she kept her back turned. Caleb saw her shoulders tense at Timothy's name.

"I should check on Margaret," she said suddenly, heading for the stairs. But Caleb caught the shine in her eyes as she passed.

After Mills left, Caleb stood at his workbench, running his hands over the half-finished wedding chest. The wood was perfect, even if the price wasn't. His fingers found each groove and joint, testing their strength. Emma appeared from behind the lumber, no longer pretending not to listen.

"Pa," she said, moving to help him clean the tools as she did every afternoon. "Tommy found deer tracks behind the workshop. Real ones."

"Did he now?" Caleb replied, handing her a cloth for the saws.

"He says they're headed west." Emma's voice was casual, but her eyes oversaw him. "Like the Petersons."

Through the window, Caleb could see Thomas demonstrating his tracking skills to Margaret, who had woken from her nap. The boy pointed excitedly at marks in the dirt while his sister clutched her doll.

He turned back to Emma and saw the understanding in her green eyes. Sometimes, he forgot she was only ten. "West is a big place," he said finally.

"Big enough for a carpenter?" she asked.

The afternoon light faded early, shadows creeping across the workshop floor like spilled stains. Through the front window, Caleb watched Morrison's Dry Goods shut its doors, though it was barely four o'clock. A hand-painted sign in the window announced reduced hours "until further notice." The third shop this week to close early.

Emma remained at the workbench, carefully arranging tools though they'd been cleaned an hour ago. Her eyes drifted to the corner where Caleb had spread the Oregon Trail maps, their creases softened by frequent handling. He'd meant to put them away before the children saw them, but Emma missed little these days.

Upstairs, Sarah's voice carried down as she counted their supplies. "Three pounds of flour, half-pound of coffee, a bit of salt pork..." A pause. "Caleb, we're lower on provisions than I thought."

He didn't answer. The maps drew his attention again – the long curve of the Platte River, the shadow of the Rocky Mountains, and the promised fertile valleys of the Willamette. His finger traced the route Timothy had marked, calculating distances, wondering if his leg would hold up to such a journey.

"Pa!" Thomas's shout broke his concentration. The boy pressed his face against the workshop window, smearing the glass. "There's another wagon passing! Bigger than the last one!"

"Don't smudge the window," Caleb called back, but Thomas had already darted away, following the wagon down the street. Through the glass, Caleb caught glimpses of household goods piled high, and children perched atop furniture, all headed west.

Margaret appeared at the top of the stairs. She settled herself in the sawdust pile, scooping handfuls and letting them fall through her fingers. "Look, Pa," she said softly. "It's snowing."

Sarah appeared behind her, a mending basket balanced on her hip. Even in the dim light, Caleb could see the worn spots on the children's clothes she carried. She set the basket down with a sigh that spoke of more than just fatigue.

"The Williams family's leaving next week," she said, watching Margaret play. "Mary Williams said they've sold everything except what fits in their wagon." She paused, then added quietly, "She asked if we wanted the first choice of what's left."

Emma's hands stilled on the tools. Thomas's face reappeared at the window, his breath fogging the glass as he strained to see the last wagon. Margaret continued playing with the sawdust, humming a tune that sounded suspiciously like "Sweet Betsy from Pike," a song they'd heard more often lately.

"What would we do with more things?" Caleb asked, his voice rougher than he intended. "Can't eat furniture."

"No," Sarah agreed softly. "But Mary's butter churn is solid oak. Could bring a good price... later."

The unspoken word hung between them: Oregon. Where butter churns and skilled carpentry might mean something again, where land waited for those brave or desperate enough to claim it.

Another shop's shutters banged closed down the street. The sound echoed through the workshop like a gunshot. Emma jumped, her elbow knocking against the carefully arranged tools. A chisel clattered to the floor, the sound sharp in the growing darkness.

"Sorry, Pa," she whispered, bending to retrieve it. But her eyes weren't on the fallen tool – they were on the map, on the extended trail west that Timothy's letter had described.

Caleb crossed to light the workshop's lamps, his leg aching after the long day of standing. The flame caught, throwing warm light across the room.

"Thomas," he called. "Come away from that window. Time to wash for supper."

The boy lingered, one finger tracing the path of the departed wagon on the glass. "Pa? Jimmy Patterson says his cousin saw real Indians in Missouri. Is that where the wagons are going?"

"Some of them," Caleb answered carefully. "Some go further."

"To Oregon?" Thomas's voice brightened. "Like the Petersons?"

Sarah's hands tightened on her mending basket. Margaret looked up from her sawdust play. Even Emma held her breath, waiting for his answer.

The evening meal was simple: cornbread and bean soup, with the last of September's preserved apples for the children. Steam rose from their bowls, carrying the sharp scent of the wild onions Sarah had traded her knitting for. The family gathered around the worn kitchen table, its surface bearing the marks of nineteen years of Wheeler family suppers.

"Reverend Mills says half the congregation's talking about Oregon now," Sarah said, breaking the silence as she served Thomas a second helping of soup. "The Blackwells sold their store today. Lock, stock, and barrel."

"Blackwells, too?" Caleb tore his cornbread slowly, watching the crumbs scatter. "That store's been there since before my father's time."

"Mary Blackwell told me they've got family in Missouri." Sarah's voice remained carefully neutral. "Said they're leaving before the first snow."

Emma stirred her soup, eyes down but ears alert. Thomas hurriedly reached for the folded newspaper beside Caleb's plate, knocking over his milk cup.

"Thomas!" Sarah moved quickly, but milk had already soaked the paper's edges.

"Sorry, Ma." Thomas righted his cup, keeping his eyes fixed on the paper. "I just wanted to see the picture of the mountains again."

Caleb patted the spill with his napkin, careful to save the newspaper.

"The Petersons wrote about real tall trees," Emma said suddenly. "And soil so rich you can grow anything."

Sarah's spoon paused halfway to her mouth. "When did you hear from the Petersons?"

Emma flushed. "I... I heard Reverend Mills telling Pa."

"Eavesdropping isn't becoming Emma Wheeler," Sarah scolded, but her heart wasn't in it. Her eyes drifted to the window, where another wagon rolled past in the gathering dusk.

"Could we grow anything, Pa?" Thomas asked. "If we had soil like that?"

The question hung in the air like wood smoke. Caleb felt Sarah's eyes on him, waiting. Even Margaret seemed to sense the moment's weight.

"Your mother could," Caleb said finally. "She's got the touch for growing things."

"But we'd need land first," Emma added quietly, her eyes meeting her father's.

Sarah set her spoon down with a sharp click. "Land we have. Right here."

"Mortgaged land," Caleb said, the words escaping before he could catch them. "With a workshop that's emptier every month."

Thomas knocked his spoon against his bowl, the rhythm matching the wagon wheels they'd heard more often lately. "Jimmy Patterson says there's buffalo out west. Whole herds of them! And Indians who teach you to track deer, and–"

"That's enough, Thomas," Sarah cut in. But Caleb saw how her hands trembled slightly as she reached for the cornbread.

"The Blackwells' store was doing better than most," Emma observed, her voice thoughtful. "If they're leaving..."

"They're chasing dreams," Sarah said firmly. "Dreams and stories about free land and fresh starts."

"Sometimes dreams are all we have left to chase," Caleb replied softly.

The silence followed was broken only by the scrape of spoons and the distant rumble of wagon wheels. Sensing the tension, Margaret reached for her doll and hugged it.

"Ma?" Thomas asked suddenly. "If we went to Oregon, could I learn to track like a real scout?"

"If we went to Oregon," Sarah's voice caught slightly, "we'd need to learn many things."

Emma's eyes darted between her parents. "Would we have to sell everything? Like the Blackwells?"

"We're not selling anything," Sarah said quickly. "We're not going anywhere." But her hand found Caleb's under the table, squeezing tight.

Caleb watched his family in the lamplight – Emma's quiet observation, Thomas's barely contained excitement, Margaret's solemn mimicry of her mother's expressions. The mortgage payment was due in two weeks, and the ledger downstairs told its own story of dwindling hopes.

After supper, Caleb made his usual workshop circuit, checking the locks twice. The night air seeped through the window frames, carrying the scent of early frost. He ached with the cold, and each step reminded him of limitations he couldn't afford to have, not if they were to...

He pushed the thought away, focusing on securing tools that grew more precious with each canceled order.

Upstairs, Sarah sat at the kitchen table by lamplight, reviewing her midwife's notebook. The page had more crossed-out appointments than confirmed ones. Her finger traced each cancellation as if searching for patterns in the loss.

"Mrs. Chen's expecting her fourth," she said without looking up. But she's going to her sister's in Pittsburgh instead. She says she can't pay anyway." Her voice carried the weight of too many similar conversations.

Emma sat cross-legged on the floor near the hearth, reading the Oregon Trail story to Thomas and Margaret. Her voice rose and fell with the tale's drama, though she'd read it so many times she hardly needed to look at the pages.

"'The wagons formed a great circle at night,'" she read, " 'like a wooden fort against the wilderness. Children slept beneath the stars while their parents planned the next day's journey across the prime farmland of the territory...'"

"What's prime farmland?" Thomas interrupted, looking up from his collection of smooth river rocks spread before him. He'd been gathering them for weeks.

"It means the soil's good for growing things," Emma explained, showing him the accompanying illustration. "See? Like these wheat fields they're passing."

Margaret crawled into Caleb's lap as he settled in his chair by the fire, her small hands patting his beard as she always did before sleep. "Papa," she whispered, "can we sleep under stars?"

Sarah paused her pencil over her notebook. Caleb felt her attention shift, though she kept her eyes down.

"It's too cold for stars tonight, little one," he answered, but Thomas was already at the window, peering up at the night sky.

"I can see some!" he exclaimed. "Right through those clouds. They're pointing west, Pa, just like the wagons!"

"Thomas Wheeler, get away from that cold window and wash for bed," Sarah said, closing her notebook with unnecessary force. "Emma, help your sister into her nightgown."

Emma carefully marked her place in the story with a pressed flower she'd been saving. "Can I read one more page? It's about to tell how they cross the rivers."

"Tomorrow," Sarah said firmly. "It's late."

Caleb prepared for sleep, checking the front door's lock a third time – a habit born of increasing desperation in the town. Through the walls, he could hear Thomas planning tomorrow's "expedition" to himself as he washed.

"'Course we'll need supplies," the boy muttered. "Rope and hardtack and maybe a real compass..."

Emma helped Margaret with her buttons, but her eyes kept straying to the window, the west road, the same road that had taken the Petersons, the Blackwells, and so many others.

Caleb caught Sarah watching him, that same look she'd worn when he'd first told her about his leg injury years ago – a mixture of worry and determination that made his heart ache.

"I'll just check the workshop once more," he said, though he'd already secured everything.

"Twice is enough," Sarah replied softly. "Some things don't get safer no matter how often you check them."

The house settled into its nighttime quiet, broken only
by the soft crackle of banking fires and the whisper
of wind through ill-fitted windows. Caleb and Sarah
spoke in hushed tones in the kitchen, their words barely
carrying any sound.

"Harrison won't be the last," Caleb said, his voice low.
"Morrison's closing early now, and the Blackwells..." He
didn't finish the thought.

Sarah steadily packed away the day's dishes. But her
movements slowed when she reached for the precious
ceramic bowl her mother had given them as a wedding
gift. Carefully, she wrapped it in a spare piece of quilting.

"Just to protect it," she said. They both knew she'd
never worried about wrapping it before.

In the children's room, Emma lay still in her bed. Her
parents' whispers reached her through the thin walls like
fragments of a puzzle she was slowly assembling.

"Timothy says the spring trains are filling fast," her
father's voice. "If we were to..."

"If," her mother repeated, the word heavy with
unspoken meaning.

Emma pulled her journal from beneath her pillow,
writing by the faint light that seeped through the cracks

in the door. "Changes coming. Pa studied the maps again today. Ma wrapped Grandmother's bowl."

Thomas stood at their bedroom window, his slight figure silhouetted against the starlit sky. He'd dragged his bed closer to the glass last week, claiming he needed to "keep watch." He pressed his nose against the cold pane, watching for wagon trains that only passed in daylight.

In her crib, Margaret slept with a handful of wood shavings clutched alongside her doll.

Sarah moved through the kitchen, opening cupboards and counting their dwindling supplies. She paused when she found a small linen bag behind the flour bin, packed with basic medical supplies and dried herbs.

"Just in case," she whispered to herself. "For emergencies."

Caleb found her there. Without words, he wrapped his arms around her from behind.

"We could wait," he said. "Try for another season."

Sarah leaned back against him, her voice barely a whisper. "And watch more families leave? Watch our children wear patches on their patches?"

"Sarah-"

"I saw you marking the calendar," she interrupted softly. "Counting weeks until spring. Counting what we could sell, what we'd need to keep."

Emma scribed quietly in her journal: "Thomas says the stars point west. Ma's been crying when she thinks we can't see."

Thomas finally slept in bed, one hand curled around a toy wagon he'd carved.

Margaret shifted in her crib, wood shavings from her tiny fingers. Her doll wore a new dress Sarah had stitched from an old apron – the good fabric saved for "later."

The workshop lamp cast a small light as Caleb worked late into the night, continuing work on the wedding chest. Harrison's daughter would be married in three weeks, half-price or not. A Wheeler's word still meant something, even if banknotes didn't.

Each stroke of the plane revealed the oak's rich grain. His grandfather had taught him to read wood like this, to feel its strength and know its purpose. But lately, all he could read was the dwindling stack of lumber against the wall, each board representing payments that might never come.

The sound of footsteps overhead told him Sarah wasn't sleeping either. She moved through their bedroom, her steps careful but purposeful. The floorboards creaked in a pattern he recognized—she was at the trunk again, the one she'd started filling with small, necessary things: a length of rope, extra buttons, and the good scissors.

Emma's candle was still burning, and its light was visible through the high window of the workshop. The scratch of her pencil carried down to him, marking memories in her journal before they could slip away. She wrote everything now as if sensing each day in Pennsylvania might be one of the last.

"'December tenth,'" she wrote, her letters careful in the dim light. "'Pa worked late again. The wedding chest is beautiful, even if Mr. Harrison won't pay full price. Thomas found more stones for his collection. He says they're the right size for crossing rivers. I don't know how he knows that.'"

A muffled thump from the children's room drew Caleb's attention. Thomas, no doubt, repositioning himself for a better view of the stars. The boy had taken to studying the night sky with the same intensity he once applied to track deer behind the workshop. "Got to learn the stars, Pa," he'd said yesterday. "For when we're on the trail."

Not if. When.

Caleb set down his plane, touching the chest's smooth surface. The wood was excellent and trustworthy. It would serve Harrison's daughter well, whatever he paid for it. But his eyes drifted to the corner where he'd stacked the pine boards he'd been saving – boards that would make a sturdy wagon bed if a man were thinking of such things.

Sarah's quiet steps descended the workshop stairs. She carried Margaret's doll, which had been dropped during some dream-driven movement. But instead of returning upstairs, she settled on the bottom step, watching him work.

"I made a list," she said, voice barely above a whisper. "Things we'd need. Things we could sell."

Caleb nodded, not trusting his voice.

"The Blackwells' store sold for enough to buy three wagons," Sarah continued. "Mary told me they're leaving before the winter storms next week."

"We'd need one wagon," Caleb said. "Maybe two." The calculations he'd been making these past weeks spilled out. "The tools we'd have to keep, the ones we could sell. The lumber we'd need for repairs along the way."

Sarah's fingers played with the edge of the doll's dress. "Emma's been reading about the trail every chance she gets. She knows more about it than she lets on."

"Thomas, too," Caleb agreed. "Been practicing his tracking, talking about rivers and mountains like he's already seen them."

"And Margaret..." Sarah's voice caught. "She asked me today if we could take the sawdust pile. Said she wants to sleep in it when we camp."

When, not if.

Caleb crossed to the workbench, retrieving Timothy's letter from its hiding place. "Spring trains forming. Good families. Three hundred and twenty acres for the claiming. Timber like you wouldn't believe."

Sarah stood, still holding the doll. Her free hand found his, solid and sure despite everything. Through the window, the stars Thomas observed wheeled above them, pointing west to lands they'd never seen.

"We'll need to tell them soon," she said softly. "Before the whole town knows."

Caleb nodded, feeling the weight and the hope of it all settling on him like sawdust after a long day's work. "Tomorrow," he said. "We'll tell them tomorrow."

2

SEEDS OF CHANGE

Pennsylvania, February 1843

The town crier's bell cut through the gray April morning, its tone sharper than the usual wake-up call. Caleb paused in the workshop doorway with his hand on the latch. The bell rang again, closer now, and Harrison's name echoed through Williamsport's muddy streets.

"Williamsport Bank closed!" The crier's voice carried above the spring rain. "All accounts frozen by order of the Philadelphia Exchange!"

Emma appeared at Caleb's elbow, clutching the bank notes from Harrison's wedding chest. The payment they'd finally extracted after months of negotiations now trembled in her tiny hands. "Pa? What does 'frozen' mean?"

Before he could answer, bodies filled the street, streaming toward the bank. Their voices rose like startled birds, carrying fragments of fear to the workshop door.

"...life savings..."

"...promised it was safe..."

"...Philadelphia says..."

Sarah's hand found his shoulder warm through his worn shirt. "The whole payment?" she asked softly.

Caleb nodded, watching Harrison's carriage appear at the bank's rear entrance. The banker's family huddled inside, trunks strapped high, facing forward as if afraid to meet the town's eyes. Three months ago, he'd told his family they'd leave for Oregon. The choice felt less like a decision now and more like a prophecy.

Thomas burst from the workshop, his wooden sword forgotten in the excitement. "Pa! Look what's flying from the bank!" The boy darted into the street, snatching at papers from Harrison's hastily emptied office.

"Thomas!" Sarah called, but he was already weaving through the crowd.

The mass of people parted briefly, revealing Mrs. Peterson collapsed on the bank's steps. Her gray hair had come loose from its usual tight bun, and her hands pressed against the locked doors as if she could force them open through will alone.

Sarah squeezed Caleb's arm once before hurrying to Mrs. Peterson's side. The midwife's instinct to help never failed, even now when her family's future lay scattered like those worthless papers in the mud.

"The Philadelphia Exchange can't do this!" Someone shouted. "We've got rights!"

Rights, Caleb thought, meant little when the money disappeared. He'd learned that lesson in '37 when the first panic hit. Watching Harrison's carriage disappear toward Philadelphia, he thanked God they'd already started selling what they could. The wagon would need more than worthless bank notes to reach Oregon.

Emma's fingers worked the edges of Harrison's payment, carefully folding the now-useless paper. "Should I add these to the tin box?" she asked. They'd been saving everything that might serve as fuel on the trail.

"Might as well," Caleb replied. "Paper's paper, whether it's worth something or not."

Thomas returned, his arms full of scattered documents. His cheeks were flushed with excitement, and mud splattered his knees. "Look what I found! Mr. Harrison's ledger pages. There are numbers bigger than I can read!"

Sarah reappeared, supporting Mrs. Peterson with one arm. The older woman's face was wet with more than rain. "She'll sit with us a while," Sarah said, "Her savings... everything she had..."

The crowd's volume rose as more carriages appeared behind the bank. Junior partners and clerks were making their escapes, Caleb realized. All headed east to Philadelphia while his family's salvation lay west. The irony might have made him laugh if he couldn't see his neighbors' dreams crumbling in the mud.

"Pa?" Emma's voice drew his attention back. She stood in the workshop doorway. "Is this why we're going to Oregon?"

Caleb met his daughter's eyes, seeing his question reflected there. Was it God's hand or simple luck that had pushed them toward this decision months ago? Either way, watching his neighbors' world collapse only confirmed what his heart had known since that first letter from Oregon.

"Part of why," he answered carefully. "But not all of it. Sometimes, the Lord closes one door to point us toward another."

When Postmaster Thompson knocked on the workshop door, Mrs. Peterson had just settled with a cup of Sarah's chamomile tea. The older man's face was flushed from more than the morning's excitement, his mail pouch clutched tight against his chest.

"Special delivery for you, Wheeler," Thompson said, pulling a thick envelope from his bag. "From Oregon Territory. Joshua Bennett's mark on it."

Caleb's hands were still rough with sawdust as he took the letter. The familiar scrawl of his old friend, the town's former blacksmith, seemed to blur before his eyes. Three months of hoping for this response, and now it sat in his callused palm.

"Mary Bennett's written in the margins," Sarah observed, appearing at his elbow. She'd developed a keen eye for such details since they'd begun corresponding with families already in Oregon. "Looks like a long letter."

Thompson lingered, shifting from foot to foot. In a town where half the storefronts now bore "Closing" signs, news from Oregon carried more weight than Sunday sermons. "Bennett doing well out there, then?"

Instead of answering, Caleb broke the seal. The pages were covered in Joshua's bold hand, with Mary's neater script flowing around the edges like a river marking new territory. His eyes caught phrases that made his throat tight: "640 acres," "timber thick as church columns," and "soil black as coffee grounds."

Emma drew closer and more attentively. Since their family meeting three months ago, she'd studied every scrap of Oregon news, building her "preparation notebook."

"Joshua says..." Caleb's voice caught. He cleared his throat and tried again. "Joshua says they've claimed a full section. Double the normal allotment on account of being married. Trees so tall you can't see their tops without craning your neck."

Sarah's hand found his arm, steadying him as she read over his shoulder. Her finger traced Mary's marginal notes about medicinal plants and wild herbs, information she'd been collecting since their decision to leave.

Thomas had abandoned his street-scattered papers to practice writing "Oregon" in the workshop's sawdust. Each letter was carefully formed, though the 'g' still troubled him. "Did Mr. Bennett see any Indians?" he asked, not looking up from his work.

"He trades with them regularly," Caleb replied, still reading. "Says they're fair dealers if you treat them with respect."

Thompson's eyebrows rose at this, but he kept his peace. The postmaster had seen too many letters flow through his office lately, all carrying the same westward dreams, to judge any man's choices.

"Mary's written about the journey," Sarah said softly, her finger moving to a heavily annotated margin. "They lost a wagon at the Snake River but saved most of their goods. Says the key is not to rush the river crossings."

Caleb nodded, remembering Joshua's strong hands at the forge and how they'd never rushed a single piece of ironwork. The man had always preached patience with crucial tasks. Now, he was preaching it again from two thousand miles west.

"Pa?" Emma's voice was careful, the same tone she'd used when they'd first discussed leaving. "Your hands are shaking."

He hadn't noticed, but she was right. The pages trembled slightly, making Joshua's bold letters dance. "Just the morning chill," he said, though they all knew better.

Sarah took the letter gently, moving to the workbench where the light was better. Her practical nature asserted itself as she began making notes: supplies they'd need, warnings to heed, skills to master before spring mud dried enough for wagon wheels.

Thomas had graduated from writing in sawdust to drawing what he imagined Oregon's mountains might look like. "Mr. Bennett probably lives in a fort," he declared. "With lookout towers for watching Indians."

"He lives in a proper house," Sarah corrected, reading from Mary's notes. "Built it himself from Oregon timber. The trees are straight as Sunday prayers and twice as tall as Williamsport's church steeple."

Caleb's hands had steadied, but his heart hadn't. Every word in Joshua's letter confirmed what they'd been planning these three months, what the bank's closure this morning had only underlined. There was nothing left for them in Williamsport but memories and mortgages.

"Thompson," he said, turning to the postmaster, who still unassumingly lingered. "You'll be seeing more letters like this, I expect. Once word of the bank gets around."

The old man nodded in agreement. "I already had three families ask about western mail rates this week, though after today..." He glanced toward the street. There might be more asking tomorrow."

When Sarah arrived, the market square was half-empty. Emma and Thomas trailed behind with their baskets. Where thirty stalls usually crowded the muddy ground, barely fifteen remained. The spring rain had slackened to a drizzle, but few shoppers braved even that to visit the depleted displays.

Sarah clutched her sewing bundle closer, the clothes she'd mended for trading feeling lighter than usual. Since their decision to leave, she'd taken on extra work, squinting by candlelight to finish seams that might be traded for supplies they'd need on the trail.

"Williams's shop is closed, Ma," Emma reported, pointing to the usually bustling general store. A rough-painted sign hung crooked on the door: "Closing After 20 Years - All Must Go."

Thomas pressed his face against Williams's window, breath fogging the glass. "There's almost nothing left inside. Just empty shelves and some barrels."

Sarah steered them toward Catherine Barrett's herb stall, where her mother's familiar figure bent over depleted baskets of dried plants. The morning's bank closure had already reached here - Sarah could read it in the tight lines around her mother's eyes.

"Supplies are low," Catherine said without preamble, gesturing to her sparse display. "Can't get half of what I need from Philadelphia anymore, and what does come costs double." She paused, watching Sarah unpack her sewing. "Those for trading?"

Sarah nodded, laying out the mended clothes. "Mrs. Thompson's shirts and the Miller children's winter things. Good work, every stitch."

"And worth half what they were yesterday," Catherine replied softly. "After the bank..." She didn't finish, but her meaning was evident in sorting through her herbs, counting and recounting dwindling stocks.

"We need potatoes," Sarah said, trying to keep her voice steady. "And salt, if anyone's still selling."

Catherine's eyes softened. "Jenkins has some potatoes left. He might trade them for mending." She added, "Mary Wilson tried paying him with bank notes this morning. He turned her away."

Thomas had wandered to the square's edge, watching another loaded wagon roll east toward Philadelphia. They'd seen three already this morning, all carrying what remained of Williamsport's wealth toward the city that had just betrayed them.

Sarah found Jenkins's stall nearly bare, but he brightened at seeing her sewing bundle. "Could use some mending done," he admitted, eyeing the neat stitches on Mrs. Thompson's shirts. "Got six potatoes left and a bit of salt, too, if you're interested."

The negotiation was quick, and both knew how little there was to bargain with. Sarah traded an hour's fine stitching for food that would have cost pennies last week. Thomas helped carry their reduced purchases, his usual chatter subdued by the market's desperate atmosphere.

"Last penny candy," the sweet-seller called halfheartedly from his cart. "Closing up after today. Everything must go."

Margaret's small face appeared in Sarah's mind - how her youngest lit up at rare treats. "Thomas," she said, pressing their final penny into his hand. "For your sister."

He clutched the coin, understanding the gesture. "I'll pick her favorite color."

Emma moved closer to Sarah as they waited, her voice low. "Ma? Are all the stores going to close?"

Before Sarah could answer, Morrison's wife hurried past, her apron still dusted with flour from the bakery. "It's finished," she announced to anyone who would listen. "First the bank, now the flour mill's shutting down. Says they can't extend credit anymore."

The news rippled through the remaining market stalls like wind through wheat. Sarah watched faces age years in moments as people calculated what it meant. No flour mill meant no bread, meant no trade, meant...

"Time to go home," she said firmly, gathering their meager purchases. But Emma's question haunted her steps. Were all the stores going to close? The answer pressed against her throat like a prayer she didn't want to voice.

Thomas returned with a single red candy, carefully wrapped in paper. "For Margaret," he said solemnly. "Because she likes the color of sunset."

Sarah nodded. "She will be pleased."

Catherine came to her side and placed a small packet of herbs into her hand. "For the journey," she whispered. "When you're ready to tell me about it."

The sound of hammering drew Caleb to his workshop window. Across the street, Cooper stood on a ladder, driving nails into a sign that would end twenty-three years of business: "Everything Must Go - Store Closing." Each strike of Cooper's hammer seemed to echo through Caleb's chest like judgment.

Three months of secret preparation hadn't softened the blow of watching his neighbors' lives splinter apart.

Cooper's Mercantile had been a fixture since before Caleb apprenticed to his father. The shop's bell had rung every morning at seven, precise as prayer.

The workshop door opened, admitting Reverend Mills and the damp April air. The preacher's collar sat askew, his usually neat appearance showing signs of a morning spent comforting parishioners outside the bank.

"Three more families," Mills said. "The Richardsons, the Hunters, and young David Porter with his new bride. All are heading west after Sunday's service."

Caleb's hands found their way to the workbench, steadying himself against the smooth oak. Behind him, Emma crept, organizing his tools with the same attention she'd given to recording market prices. Each chisel and plane lay precisely in place as if proper order could hold their world together.

"Porter just married last month," Caleb said, watching Cooper's sign tilt in the spring wind.

"Started their life with bank notes that aren't worth the paper they're printed on." Mills shook his head. "At least in Oregon, a man's work means something. Land for the taking, timber for the cutting."

In the corner, Thomas had created an elaborate sawdust trail with wooden block mountains and twine rivers. His voice carried soft as he played: "The wagons ford here, where the water's lowest..."

Margaret sat amid her creation - wood scraps arranged in careful peaks and valleys. Her small hands shaped the pieces with surprising care, mimicking the mountains she'd heard so much about these past months.

The workshop door opened again, bringing Sarah back from the market. Her basket sat lighter than it should, but her eyes were heavy. She paused at the sight of Reverend Mills, reading the news in his presence.

"How many?" she asked.

"Three families, so far," Mills replied. "Though after Cooper's sign goes up..." He let the thought hang unfinished.

Caleb found Joshua's letter in his pocket. The pages spelled out hope in ink and paper: fertile soil, abundant timber, and a fresh start. He spread it on the workbench, where Emma's careful organization left clean space.

"Says here Bennett's already added a smithy to his claim," he said, finger tracing the lines. "Trading with settlers up and down the valley. Man who could work wood would find plenty of business."

Sarah moved to stand beside him, her hand finding his shoulder. She smelled of market mud and penny candy - Margaret's treat carefully wrapped in her basket. "Cooper's sign is crooked," she observed softly.

"Man never could drive a nail straight," Caleb replied, the familiar criticism carrying years of neighborly history. "Always came to me for his display shelves."

Emma had started a new page in her notebook, recording the names Mills had brought. Her pen scratched quietly: Richardson, Hunter, Porter. Then, after a pause, Cooper. She looked up at her father, question in her eyes.

"Add Williams," Sarah said, unpacking her thin purchases. "And Morrison's bakery, soon enough."

Thomas abandoned his sawdust trail to press his face against the window, watching Cooper descend his ladder. "How many wagons would it take, Pa? For all of them?"

"More than the town has horses to pull," Mills answered for him. "Some will go east to family in Philadelphia or New York. Some will stay, trying to rebuild." He paused, eyes moving to Joshua's letter. "And some will look west."

Margaret had completed her mountain range, placing a small wooden figure - one of Caleb's test pieces - at its peak. "House," she declared proudly. "Our house."

Sarah's hands stilled on her market basket. They hadn't told Margaret about Oregon, not directly. But children absorb truth like wood absorbs stains, taking it deep into the grain.

There were three months of planning in secret, of selling what they could without raising questions, of Sarah's extra sewing and Emma's careful lists. Cooper's sign creaked across the street, asking a question they'd already answered.

Sarah stretched the soup with extra dumplings, as she'd learned to do since they'd started setting aside money for the west journey. Steam rose from the bowls, carrying the scent of the few vegetables she'd managed to trade for at the market. The family gathered around their kitchen table, its scarred surface, witnessing another meal that felt more like a council of war.

Caleb unfolded Joshua's letter beside his bowl, its pages marked with afternoon readings. "Bennett writes that spring trains are already gathering in Independence," he said, voice carefully neutral. "Says the grass turns green there weeks before it does here."

Emma's notebook lay open beside her bowl, columns of figures marching down the page. Her soup cooled untouched as she calculated. "If we sold the lathe," she said softly, "and maybe the new saw set..."

"Eat your soup," Sarah interrupted, though her eyes lingered on Emma's figures. They'd all become accountants of necessity these past months, weighing the value of every possession against miles of prairie crossing.

Thomas broke his dumpling into pieces, arranging them like stepping stones across his bowl. "Jimmy Patterson says his uncle was a scout in Missouri. He says he learned to track buffalo and speak Indian languages and–"

"James Patterson fills your head with tales," Sarah said, but without heat. They'd all clung to tales of the west lately, weighing them against Williamsport's crumbling certainties.

Margaret built a wagon from her bread crust, with tiny wheels pressed into the soft dough. She rolled it across the table's edge, humming softly to herself.

Caleb watched his family's quiet industry—Emma's calculations, Thomas's plotting, Margaret's innocent play. This morning, the bank's closure confirmed what they'd known since winter: Williamsport was dying by inches. Their prayers felt different lately, heavy with questions about providence and promise.

"Joshua says..." Caleb paused, gathering his thoughts. "Says a man who knows timber could build more than a living out there. Could build a future."

Sarah's spoon hesitated over her bowl. "Mary Bennett writes that they lost two months' worth of supplies crossing the Snake River. You can't trust its mood from one hour to the next."

"Which is why we prepare," Emma said, tapping her pencil against the notebook. "If we pack the wagon right, distribute the weight properly..." She'd been studying wagon loading since their decision, questioning every trader who passed through town.

"I could help scout river crossings," Thomas offered, sitting straighter. "I've been practicing tracking in the workshop yard, and-"

"You'll be helping your mother," Caleb said firmly. "All of you will. The trail's no place for adventures."

Margaret pushed her bread wagon across the table toward Oregon, or at least toward where Oregon would be if their family Bible's map had been open. "When do we go?" she asked.

The question stilled all motion at the table. They hadn't spoken of it openly before, not with Margaret present. But children knew, as Sarah always said. They knew in their bones when change was coming.

Sarah reached for Caleb's hand under the table, her fingers strong and sure despite the tremor in her voice. "We should tell them properly," she said. "All of it."

Caleb nodded, finally feeling the mass of three months' planning settle into words. "Your mother and I..." he began, then stopped, starting again. "This morning's news from the bank... it only confirms what we've been preparing for."

Emma paused her writing. Thomas abandoned his dumpling trail. Even Margaret sensed the moment's importance, her bread-wagon forgotten.

"Come spring," Caleb continued, "when the roads are firm enough for wagons, we'll leave Williamsport. Going to Oregon Territory, where the Bennetts are. Where there's land for those willing to work it, timber for those who know how to use it."

The words hung in the steam rising from their bowls, mixing with the evening shadows gathering in the kitchen corners. Sarah's hand tightened on his.

"We've been getting ready," Emma said. "Haven't we? That's why we've been selling things, why Ma's been taking in extra sewing."

Thomas's eyes shone with barely contained excitement. "Will we see Indians? And buffalo? And mountains tall as clouds?"

"We'll see hard work," Sarah answered honestly. "Long days of walking beside the wagon, dust that gets into everything, rivers that need crossing whether we're ready or not."

Margaret pushed her bread wagon toward Caleb. "Can we take the workshop?" she asked, her tiny voice carrying all the innocence they'd tried to protect.

Emma found her mother in the bedroom after supper, drawn by muffled sounds that might have been crying. The door stood ajar, lamplight spilling across scattered daguerreotypes spread on her parents' bed. Sarah sat amid the images, her braid coming loose, fingers tracing faces frozen in silver.

"Ma?" Emma hesitated at the threshold, caught between childhood's instinct to retreat from adult pain and her growing sense of responsibility.

Sarah looked up, hastily wiping her eyes. "Come in, Emma. Help me wrap these properly." A piece of quilting lay ready, cut from Sarah's first attempt at patchwork. "They'll need protection on the journey."

Emma crossed to the bed, careful not to disturb the arranged portraits. She recognized faces: grandparents, aunts, uncles, cousins who'd posed stiffly for the traveling photographer last summer. She found a smaller image, separate from the others.

"Baby James," Sarah said softly—her brother who'd lived six days, long enough only for one picture. Emma remembered the fever that took him and how the house had gone quiet as Sunday afternoon.

"Should we pack them in order?" Emma asked, reaching for her notebook. "By family, maybe, or by-"

"No." Sarah's voice caught. "No lists for this, Emma. Some things we do by heart."

The quilting was soft under Emma's fingers as she helped wrap the first portrait - Grandmother Barrett in her midwife's apron, herbs hanging behind her. The same apron now held different herbs chosen for a journey west.

"Your grandmother's remedy book," Sarah nodded toward the leather-bound volume beside her. She had brought it from England as a girl. It was the first thing she packed when they crossed the ocean." She paused, touching the book's worn cover. "I used to think that was the furthest anyone could travel."

Emma spotted her photograph among the others – last year's birthday portrait- standing straight behind the workshop door. "We'll take pictures in Oregon," she offered. "Send them back to everyone so they can see–"

"See what we've left behind?" Sarah's words carried no bitterness, only a weight Emma was learning to recognize. "See what we're trading for Bennett's promised land?"

Movement in the doorway drew their attention. Margaret stood there in her nightgown, "Mama? Are you crying?"

Sarah beckoned her youngest closer. "Just remembering, little one. Come see these pictures before we wrap them up."

Margaret climbed onto the bed, careful of the portraits arranged like cards in a game none of them quite knew how to play. Her tiny finger found Baby James's image. "He looks like Thomas," she said.

"Yes." Sarah's voice steadied. "He had the Wheeler eyes."

Emma watched her mother gather Margaret close, showing her the faces they'd leave behind. She explained who smiled from each silver surface, what made them family, and how they'd carry these memories west.

The room grew darker as their lamp burned low, shadows gathering in corners where familiar furniture would soon be sold. Emma's fingers found her notebook's outline pressing through her apron pocket. She'd listed everything else about their preparation, but as her mother said, some things had to be done by heart.

Sarah reached for another piece of quilting and stopped. "Emma? The first story I heard about Oregon; do you want to know what it was?"

Emma nodded, settling closer.

"I was carrying you, just newly sure about it. Your father came home talking about timber and acres and how a man could build something lasting out there." Sarah smoothed the quilting across her lap. "I told him we had something lasting right here. I told him our family was rooted deep as the workshop's foundation."

"What changed your mind?"

"You did. The day you were born, looking up at me with your father's eyes, I understood about wanting to build something lasting." Sarah's fingers found Baby James's portrait again. "Understood protecting what matters, even if it means leaving what's familiar."

Margaret had dozed off against her mother's side, one hand still touching a picture of Grandfather Wheeler at his forge. Sarah carefully lifted the portrait away, beginning to wrap it.

"I was going to write everything down," Emma admitted. "Make lists of who's in each picture, where they were taken, when—"

"Some things we carry deeper than paper, Emma." Sarah passed her a portrait to wrap. "Like how your grandmother's hands move when sorting herbs or your father tests wood grain with his thumbs. Those memories don't need lists."

Catherine Barrett's cottage sat at the edge of town, its herb garden still sleeping under the mud. Sarah approached through the morning mist drawn by the lamp burning in her mother's window. The invitation had come with last night's market herbs: "Come early. There are things you need to know."

The cottage door opened before she could knock. Catherine stood outlined against the warmth, her apron already tied on despite the early hour. "Your father was the same way," she said in greeting. "Night before he left for the sea. Couldn't sleep then, either."

Sarah followed her mother inside, where familiar bundles of drying herbs hung from the rafters. The cottage air carried decades of healing: chamomile for fevers, yarrow for wounds, willow bark for pain. Each scent marked a lesson learned at her mother's side.

"Sit," Catherine ordered, moving to the corner where her medicine chest stood. The box was made of ancient oak, brought from England by her grandmother. Sarah had never seen it open fully; she only glimpsed its contents when her mother retrieved specific remedies.

Today, Catherine threw back the lid without ceremony. "You'll need to know everything," she said, her voice practical despite the tremor in her hands. "The trail won't wait for a proper apprenticeship."

Through the cottage's back window, Sarah caught movement. Emma's shape was darker against the dawn, watching from the herb garden. Of course, she'd followed—the girl missed nothing these days.

Catherine began pulling out packets and bottles, her movements quick but precise. "Yarrow, you know, and chamomile. Good for trail fevers. But here..." She extracted a leather-bound book from the chest's bottom drawer. "Your grandmother's remedies. The ones that don't grow in gardens."

The book's pages carried four generations of women's writing and recipes annotated in different hands. Sarah recognized some of these from her training: wound poultices, fever teas, and birth medicines. But others...

"Trading remedies," Catherine explained, pointing to a section marked with red thread. "What plants to watch for past the Mississippi. What the natives use for snake bite, grass fever, and births gone wrong." Her finger traced a carefully drawn leaf. "This one grows all along the trail. Mary Bennett mentioned it in her letter."

Sarah's throat tightened. "How did you know about Mary's letter?"

"Mothers know, girl. As you know, Emma was listening from the garden before I mentioned her." Catherine's voice carried years of wisdom learned between heartbeats. "Some things we know in our bones."

The leather book creaked as Catherine turned its pages. "Your grandmother wrote these when she crossed the ocean. Sea remedies, mostly, but the principle's the same. Long journey, unknown dangers, children to protect."

Emma continued taking notes from the garden, no doubt recording everything she could see through the window. Sarah remembered being that age, watching her mother treat patients, learning which herbs meant healing and which meant last rites.

Catherine pulled out a small packet of seeds, their paper wrapper marked with careful symbols. "These don't grow in Pennsylvania," she said. "Trade goods, from before the bank's paper meant anything. They'll grow wherever you settle if you plant them right."

"Mom..." Sarah started, but Catherine shook her head.

"No time for that now. Watch here - this is how you wrap herbs for travel. They'll need to last months, maybe longer." Her hands demonstrated how to layer dried leaves between clean cloths. "And here's how you know which plants to trust when you find them. See these leaf patterns? Nature marks her medicines if you know how to look."

The morning light strengthened, casting Emma's shadow longer across the herb garden. Sarah watched her daughter sketch the plants she could recognize, preparing in her way for what lay ahead.

"You'll need a proper medicine chest," Catherine continued. "Not this old thing - too heavy for a wagon. But I've had Thomas Cooper working on one since winter. Light wood, tight joints, space for everything you'll need." She paused, her hands stilling on a bundle of herbs. "He finished it yesterday. Last thing before he put up his closing sign."

Sarah's surprise must have shown because Catherine smiled - a quick, sad expression. "Mothers know, girl. We see which way the wind blows. Why else would I have ordered that chest months ago?"

Rain fell steady as Caleb walked the three miles to his parents' farm, each step marking time with the ache in his right leg. The muddy road remembered his childhood feet, though tonight it felt longer than when he'd run it as a boy, eager to show his father each new woodworking skill.

The Wheeler farmhouse emerged from the darkness like a memory taking shape. Light burned in the front window - they'd been expecting him. His father always said bad news traveled ahead of the messenger, and today's bank closure would have reached them by sunset.

William Wheeler stood on the porch, his carpenter's frame straight despite his years. He'd taught Caleb every piece of their craft: how to read grain, feel the hidden strength in timber, and build things that would outlast their maker.

"Thought you'd come tonight," William said as Caleb climbed the steps. No other greeting was needed between them. "Your mother's got supper waiting."

Martha Wheeler worked at the kitchen table, her hands working fresh dough. The house smelled of fresh bread and coffee - comfort food for difficult conversations. She didn't look up as they entered, but her shoulders carried the tension of waiting.

"Bank's finished, then?" William settled into his chair, the one he'd made when Caleb was born. "Cooper's boy rode out to tell us about the sign he's putting up."

Caleb nodded, accepting coffee from his mother. Martha's hands never stopped kneading, though her dough had long since been worked smooth.

"Joshua Bennett wrote," Caleb said finally. The words fell into the kitchen's quiet like stones into still water. "There's timber in Oregon valleys that'd make a carpenter weep."

William's eyes went to the family Bible on its shelf, which had recorded five generations of Wheeler births, marriages, and deaths—all in Pennsylvania soil, all within reach of this kitchen.

Martha's hands stilled on her dough. Sarah's mother sent word. She said she's been teaching her trail medicines."

There was no judgment in her voice, just understanding. "She said the children are already preparing."

"Emma keeps lists," Caleb admitted. "Thomas practices knots. Even Margaret..." He didn't finish. They didn't need to, with parents who'd raised him to read the signs in wood grain and weather.

William stood, his chair scraping against worn floorboards. The Bible came down from its shelf, pages falling open to the family records. Candlelight caught the careful script of names and dates, each a story of Wheelers who'd stayed, built, and put down roots in Pennsylvania earth.

"Your grandfather brought these tools from England," William said, gesturing to the walls where ancient planes and saws hung like family portraits. "Said American timber needed English steel to shape it properly." He paused, running one hand along the Bible's leather spine. "Never thought to ask him if he missed English timber after he crossed."

Martha wiped flour from her hands, finally meeting Caleb's eyes. "How long have you and Sarah been planning?"

"Since early winter," Caleb answered. There is no point hiding it now. "Since Thomas Cooper first mentioned closing, Harrison started talking about reduced payments."

"Three months." William's voice carried no accusation, only the careful measurement he used when testing wood.

"At the same time, I noticed tools missing from the workshop. Ones you'd need for wagon work, for trail repairs."

Caleb's throat tightened. Of course, his father had noticed that William Wheeler could spot a missing nail in a barn wall. "Didn't know how to tell you," he admitted. "How to say we're taking your grandchildren two thousand miles west when you've never been further than Pittsburgh."

Martha moved to the stove, pulling out bread that filled the kitchen with fresh warmth. Her hands shook slightly as she set it on the table. "Children go where life leads them," she said softly. "My mother said the same when I married your father and moved from Lancaster County."

"Bit further than Lancaster to Oregon," William observed, but his voice had softened. The Bible lay open between them, its pages waiting for new entries, new stories of Wheelers who'd chosen to seek rather than stay.

"I'd take the tools," Caleb said quickly. "The ones from England. Keep them in the family, pass them down to Thomas when–"

"When he's ready," William finished. "When he's learned what his father knows about reading timber, testing joints, and building things that last." The old carpenter's eyes met his son's across the kitchen table. "Might take a while, out there in Oregon territory. Might need his teacher close by."

Morning light found the Wheeler household in careful motion, each member moving to their rhythm of preparation. Sarah stood in the kitchen, copper pot in hand, counting supplies aloud as if the numbers might change with each tally.

"Three pounds of coffee... six pounds of salt... dried beans enough for..." Her voice trailed off as she marked each item in her ledger, the same book that had once held midwife appointments now recording survival materials.

In the workshop, Caleb's hands moved over tools with new purpose, sorting what they'd need from what they could sell. Each item weighed twice in his mind - once for its value in coins, once for its worth on the trail. The fine-set saw might bring enough for wagon wheels, but would they need it for building in Oregon?

Emma had taken over the parlor floor, carefully spreading clothes. Her notebook lay open beside her, each column marked with deliberate categories: "Must Take," "Can Sell," and "Will Need." Thomas's outgrown shirts went to one pile, Margaret's winter clothes to another.

"The green dress," Sarah called from the kitchen. "The one with the covered buttons. Set it aside for trading - good work brings good value out west."

At the workbench, Thomas practiced his knots with scraps of rope; his tongue caught between his teeth in concentration. "Mr. Cooper showed me this one," he announced to no one. "Says it's for securing wagon loads on steep trails."

Margaret moved between them like a butterfly, touching each pile, tool, and preparation. Her small hands gathered wood shavings into her apron, building nest after nest in corner after corner. "For remembering," she explained when Sarah asked, though what she meant to remember remained her secret.

The knock at the door came just as Sarah finished her inventory. Catherine Barrett entered without waiting for a welcome, her arms full of the promised medicine chest. The wood gleamed with fresh polish, Cooper's last masterwork before closing his shop.

"Thomas Cooper says to tell you he added a false bottom," Catherine said, setting the chest on the kitchen table. "For special medicines that need extra care." Her eyes met Sarah's. "For the ones we discussed."

Sarah's hands moved over the chest's smooth surface, finding the hidden catch just where Cooper had promised. The false bottom revealed itself with a whisper of well-fitted joints, showing the space where her mother's most precious remedies would travel.

"Emma," Catherine called. "Come see how this opens. You'll need to know if your mother's attending a birth when it's needed."

Emma appeared from her clothing piles, notebook ready. Her grandmother's lessons had taken on new urgency since the bank's closure, since Oregon had become unavoidable rather than possible.

Thomas abandoned his ropes to watch Catherine demonstrate the chest's secrets. "Like a puzzle box," he observed, fingers itching to try the mechanism himself.

"Like wisdom," Catherine corrected. "Hidden until needed, but always there if you know where to look."

The first items were already being sold quietly and carefully. Sarah's prized tea set, a wedding gift from her aunt, had gone to the minister's wife that morning. The money lay wrapped in cloth in Sarah's sewing basket, the first coins in their travel fund.

Caleb emerged from the workshop, sawdust in his beard, to find his family gathered around Catherine's medicine chest. The sight stopped him - four generations of knowledge passing down in one kitchen.

"We'll need to pack it properly," Sarah said, asserting her practical nature. "Heavier items below, delicate things cushioned, everything labeled so Emma can find what's needed quickly."

"I've made a list," Emma offered, holding up
her notebook. "From Mary Bennett's letter - which
medicines they used most on the trail."

Catherine's hand found her granddaughter's shoulder.
"Lists are good," she said. "But remember what I taught
you about reading signs. Sometimes, the trail tells you
what's needed before the list does."

Margaret had created a new nest beneath the kitchen
table, lined with scraps from Emma's clothing piles. She
hummed as she worked, a tune that sounded like the
hymns they sang on Sundays but with words of her own
making about wagons, mountains, and new places to
build nests.

Thomas returned to his ropes, but now his knots had
a purpose—each one carefully tied and tested against the
weight it might need to hold. Cooper's lessons took root
in small hands that would soon help secure their lives to
a wagon.

Reverend Mills called the town meeting for noon,
though the church bell rang hollow over streets already
changed by morning. Caleb watched from his workshop
as neighbors filed past, their faces carrying yesterday's
bank closure like a physical weight.

"Special meeting," Thomas reported from his window post. "Jimmy Patterson says his pa says it's about who's leaving and who's staying."

Emma recorded everything now—who sold what, who planned to leave, and who might have wagons to spare. The sound mixed with Sarah's footsteps overhead as she prepared for what would likely be her last midwife call in Williamsport.

The workshop door opened, admitting a stream of desperate customers. Jacob Turner with his broken chair, Mary Wilson clutching her husband's only saw, old Pete Murphy carrying shutters that needed mending before winter. They all held the same knowledge in their eyes - Caleb Wheeler wouldn't be here to fix things much longer.

"Just a loose joint," Turner said, holding his chair like an offering. "Wouldn't ask, with everything happening, but my Martha's expecting and needs a place to sit properly."

Caleb took the chair, fingers finding the weakness without needing to look. Five generations of Wheelers had mended Turner furniture, each repair adding to a ledger of community that couldn't be measured in bank notes.

"I'll need it back before..." Turner's voice faded. "Before you..."

"It'll be ready tomorrow," Caleb promised, reaching for his glue pot. The work would delay his preparations, but some debts went deeper than time.

Sarah appeared in the doorway, her midwife's bag packed for Mrs. Chen's delivery. Her eyes met Caleb's. "The baby's coming early," she said. "Like it knows, times are changing."

Emma looked up from her notebook. "Do you want me to come? I could help with–"

"Stay with your father," Sarah interrupted gently. "There'll be other births to attend out west."

Through the window came the sound of scuffling – Thomas in the street, facing Billy Cooper's boy. Words drifted in: "Fever dreamers," "fool's journey," and "running away." Then, the solid thud of fists meeting flesh.

Caleb moved quickly, but Sarah reached the street first. She separated the boys, though Thomas's eye already showed signs of darkening.

"Fighting won't change what's coming," she told them both, her midwife's voice carrying calm authority. "And it won't make staying any easier for those who can't go."

Billy Cooper's split lip trembled. "Pa says only fools chase Oregon dreams. Says smart folks go east to Philadelphia."

"Your pa's welcome to his opinion," Sarah replied, but her eyes found Caleb's over the boys' heads. They'd expected this – the community fracturing along the lines of hope and fear, dreams and practicality.

Margaret appeared at the workshop door. She watched her brother's swelling eye and then offered her doll to Billy Cooper. "For sad," she explained.

The gesture broke something in the street's tension. Mary Wilson laughed softly, though it caught like a sob in her throat. "Out of the mouths of babes," she said, wiping her eyes with her apron.

Sarah shouldered her midwife's bag, pausing to kiss Margaret's head. "I'll be back before supper," she said. "Emma, mind your sister. Thomas, ice on that eye. Caleb..." She didn't finish, but her hand brushed his arm.

The workshop was filled and emptied throughout the afternoon, with neighbors bringing broken things that needed fixing or standing in the dust-scented air that had meant stability for so long. Emma recorded each visitor in her notebook as if keeping track of goodbyes already beginning.

"Your father built this cradle," Mrs. Peterson said, running her hand along the wooden rim. "And his father built the one that rocked him. Seems wrong, somehow, that my grandchildren won't have a Wheeler to mend their children's furniture."

Evening settled over the Wheeler kitchen like dust after sawing, each mote carrying the weight of the day's events. Caleb spread the Oregon Trail map across the table. Sarah had returned from Mrs. Chen's delivery, her midwife's bag lighter by several precious herbs she'd never see payment for. Some debts, she'd said, were settled in blessings rather than coins.

"Everyone sit," Caleb said, his voice carrying the same tone he used when testing wood grain - careful, measuring, sure. The family gathered around the table, even Margaret sensing the moment's gravity enough to settle without protest.

Thomas's eye had darkened to purple, but he sat straighter for it as if the bruise was a badge earned in service of their coming journey. Emma carefully positioned her notebook and pencil, ready to record this council like all the others.

Sarah lit the lamp, its glow catching the map's rivers and mountains, turning them to gold and shadow. Her hands still carried traces of new life from Mrs. Chen's delivery, the last Williamsport child she'd help bring into the world.

"We've been preparing for months," Caleb began, his finger finding Independence, Missouri on the map. "Selling what we could, learning what we must. But after the bank closure, after Cooper's sign went up..." He paused, meeting each family member's eyes in turn. "It's time to speak plain about what's coming."

Emma scribed her father's words even as she added her own carefully researched facts. "The spring trains leave Independence in early April," she said. "We'll need to leave here by mid-March to reach them in time."

"Six weeks," Sarah added softly. "Six weeks to sell everything we can't carry, say goodbye to everyone we've known, and leave the only home our children have ever known."

Thomas spread his collection of rope knots on the table, each labeled in his improving hand. "I've been practicing," he said. "Cooper showed me how to secure wagon loads, and Jimmy Patterson's uncle told me about river crossings."

"And fighting," Sarah observed, touching his swollen eye gently.

"Billy Cooper needed teaching," Thomas muttered without real anger. "He said we were running away."

Margaret carefully placed her doll on Independence, Missouri. "Doll wants to go," she announced. Then, with the innocence of her three years, she added, "Everyone wants to go."

Caleb's hand found Sarah's under the table, sharing strength as they had since their wedding day. "Not everyone can go," he corrected gently. "Some will stay, try to rebuild. Some will go east to Philadelphia or New York. But we..." He took a deep breath. "We're going to Oregon Territory. To the Willamette Valley, where Joshua Bennett says 'timber grows tall as church steeples and soil runs black as coffee grounds.'"

Emma's notebook already had lists of what they'd need: wagons, oxen, and supplies for six months' journey. She'd calculated costs to the last penny, accounting for every nail and yard of cloth. "I've been studying Mary Bennett's letters," she said. "About what to pack, what to expect on the trail."

"It won't be easy," Sarah added, her midwife's practicality showing through. "Disease follows wagon trains like wolves follow buffalo. We'll need every remedy Mother's taught me and probably some she hasn't."

Thomas traced the trail's path with his finger, touching each river crossing. "But we'll have adventures," he said, excitement bleeding through his careful attempt at maturity. "See real Indians, buffalo, and mountains taller than anything in Pennsylvania."

"We'll have each other," Caleb corrected. "Family stays together on the trail, Thomas. No wandering off, no matter what wonders appear."

Margaret had begun arranging her wooden blocks along the trail, building little houses regularly. "For resting," she explained when they all looked at her. "When legs get tired."

Dawn hadn't touched the workshop windows when Caleb nailed the notice to his door. His hammer struck with practiced care, each blow measured as if setting joints in fine furniture rather than posting the end of five generations of Wheeler woodworking in Williamsport.

WHEELER WORKSHOP - CLOSING

All Tools and Timber for Sale

Inquire Within

The letters stood stark against the white paper, black as the coffee Sarah had pressed into his hands before he'd come down. Strangely, such small words could carry the burden of many years and decisions.

Sarah appeared at his elbow, her task completed - a letter to Joshua Bennett accepting his invitation to join them in Oregon's Willamette Valley. The pages sat sealed in her hand, ready for Thompson to carry west with tomorrow's mail.

"It's done then," she said softly, watching him step back from the notice.

Emma worked at her desk by lamplight, pen scratching across paper as she composed farewell letters to her friends. Her careful script carried none of the tremors that had shaken her hand when they'd first discussed leaving, and three months of preparation had turned fear into purpose.

"Dear Mary," she wrote, "By the time you read this, we'll be preparing the wagon. Mother says we can't take much, but I'm pressing flowers from the garden to remember Pennsylvania by. Perhaps you could press some too, and we could compare them when we write..."

Thomas knelt in the workshop yard, morning dew soaking his knees as he buried his treasure box. Inside, he'd placed his most precious possessions: a perfect arrowhead found behind the church, his grandfather's brass compass, and a map of their street drawn in his hand.

"For coming back," he whispered as he smoothed dirt over his cache. "Someday."

Margaret sat in the kitchen with her mother's worn Bible open before her. Sarah showed her how to avoid damaging the delicate paper, teaching their youngest that even remembrances needed careful handling.

Heavy steps on the workshop porch announced William and Martha Wheeler's arrival. Caleb's parents carried more than themselves across the threshold—William's arms cradled a wooden chest wrapped in oilcloth, while Martha held a smaller box close to her heart.

"Your grandfather's tools," William said, setting the chest down with the reverence reserved for holy things. "English steel for American timber." He paused, running one hand along the chest's smooth oak. "Or Oregon timber, as it may be."

Martha opened her box, revealing the gleam of well-kept brass and steel. "For Thomas," she said. "Your father's first set of carpenter's apprentice tools. Seems fitting they should travel west with their namesake."

Sarah's hands found her mother's medicine chest, its new wood bright against the workshop's aged beams—three generations of healing knowledge packed into Cooper's last masterwork. "We'll need everything," she said softly. "Every tool, every remedy, every bit of wisdom we can carry."

Emma appeared with her stack of farewell letters, each sealed with a pressed flower from the garden. Her eyes caught on her grandfather's chest of tools, understanding flowing across her face as she added another line to her notebook: "Family travels in more than wagons."

Thomas burst in from the yard, dirt still fresh under his fingernails from burying his treasures. The sight of his grandmother holding apprentice tools stopped him mid-stride, his bruised eye forgotten in the moment of inheritance.

"Come here, boy," William said gruffly. "Let me show you how these fit your hands."

Margaret drew everyone's attention as she carefully closed the Bible around Miss Liberty. "She's ready," she announced. "For Oregon."

Caleb stood in his workshop doorway, watching his family gather around the tools and treasures that would travel west with them. The notice behind him caught the rising sun, its shadow stretching across five generations of sawdust and wood shavings.

Sarah stepped close, her letter to Joshua Bennett still in hand. "No turning back now," she whispered.

"No," he agreed. "But we go together."

They could see Cooper's sign across the street through the window, the early light catching its fresh paint. Other notices would follow - the Williams store, Morrison's bakery, and the bank's final closure. But the Wheelers had already turned their faces west, toward tall timber and rich soil, toward Oregon Territory, and whatever waited beyond the edge of their known world.

3

THE WEIGHT OF LEGACY

Pennsylvania, February 1843

Thunder cracked over Williamsport. Through the workshop's window, Caleb watched his father stroll towards him. One hand gripped his walking stick; the other clutched something against his coat.

Three days had passed since they'd posted the workshop's closing notice. The sign hung limp now.

William Wheeler didn't knock. Water dripped from his coat onto a floor that no longer needed sweeping.

"Thought I'd find you here," William said. "Despite that sign you've hung." He pulled a folded newspaper from beneath his coat, already opening to a marked page. "Thought you should see this before you sell everything your grandfather built."

Caleb recognized the paper - last week's Missouri Gazette, the same one that had been circulating through town since the bank closed. But William's weathered finger pointed to a different article than the usual ones about free land and timber-rich valleys.

"'Third wagon train loses twelve souls crossing the Platte,'" William read, his voice as steady as when he'd taught Caleb to saw straight. "'Among the dead, four children under the age of ten.'" He looked up, eyes finding the corner where James's cradle still stood, draped now in canvas for the coming sale. "Children the age of your Emma. Your Thomas."

"I've read the papers, Father." Caleb moved to check a crate of chisels, more to avoid his father's gaze than from any real need. "All of them. The good news and the bad."

"Have you?" William pulled more clippings from his coat. "Have you read about the cholera? The broken axles that strand families in Indian territory? The rivers that rise in the night and take wagons, stock, children-"

"I've read them." Caleb's voice came sharper than he'd intended. His leg ached with the storm, making him brace against the workbench. "Just like I've read Harrison's ledger showing what he still owes for Katherine's chest. Like I've counted the empty pages in my order book."

William's eyes moved to Caleb's leg, to the slight shift in stance that showed its weakness. "That leg won't thank you for two thousand miles of prairie." He paused, then added quietly, "Neither will Sarah if something happens to the children."

"You think I haven't thought of that?" Caleb turned to face his father entirely. "Think I haven't measured every risk against what's happening here? Cooper's closed. The bank's gone. Williams sold his store for wagon money yesterday." He gestured to the window, where rain masked the empty storefronts across the street. "Even Harrison's daughter's wearing a second-hand wedding dress now."

William set his clippings on the workbench. "I tried it once," he said finally. "The Western Journey. The year before you were born."

"Got as far as Ohio with your mother's brother. Had all the same dreams - free land, a fresh start, a fortune for the taking. Lost the wagon in the mud. Lost our supplies to thieves. Nearly lost your mother's brother to fever." He looked up. "Crawled back to Pennsylvania with nothing but shame and a story about why a man ought to stay where his roots are planted."

A farmhand's shape appeared through the rain-streaked glass, running toward the workshop with a letter held above his head. William recognized the boy—Matthew, from their farm, barely older than Emma. The door burst open with a gust of wet wind.

"Mrs. Wheeler sent this," Matthew gasped, holding out the rain-spotted envelope. "Says it's urgent, Mr. Wheeler."

William took the letter, nodding for the boy to wait out the storm. Martha's handwriting crossed the paper in the same careful strokes she'd used to teach Caleb his letters. The sheet trembled slightly in William's hands as he read.

"Your mother's been corresponding with women back east," he said finally. "Women who watched their families leave for Oregon." His voice dropped. "Women who never heard from them again."

Caleb's fingers found a smooth piece of oak, one he'd been saving for Thomas's eighth birthday - old habit now, reaching for wood when words grew difficult. "And how many never heard from the ones who went to Philadelphia? Or New York? Or any other place people go when their town dies around them?"

Thunder punctuated his question. Matthew huddled near the door, watching grandfather and son face each other across generations of sawdust.

"Your grandfather built this workshop," William said, gesturing to the walls that had weathered sixty Pennsylvania winters. "Built it right so that it would last. So his children's children would have something solid to inherit."

"And his children's children are inheriting a town where banks close, where skilled work brings half price, where-" Caleb stopped, his leg trembling with the effort of standing straight. "Where a man can't support his family with honest craft anymore."

William's eyes caught on the leg's weakness. "That injury-"

"Will heal as well on the trail as it does here." But Caleb's hand found the workbench again, betraying the lie. "Sarah's mother's teaching her trail medicine. Emma's studying every book she can find about the journey. Even Thomas-"

"Thomas is seven," William cut in. "Playing at adventure because he's too young to understand what's at stake." He moved to the draped cradle, one hand resting on its curved edge. "Like James was too young to understand why fever took him instead of one of us."

The name fell between them like a dropped tool. Caleb's fingers tightened on the oak until its grain nearly broke the skin. "You think I don't see him? Every time I look at Margaret, every time I watch Sarah check the children for fever? You think I don't know what we're risking?"

"Then why risk it?" William's voice carried the same tone he'd used to teach Caleb to test wood. "The farm's large enough for two families. Your mother and I aren't getting younger. The land could be yours, all of it, if you'd just-"

"Stay?" Caleb's laugh held no humor. "Watch my children inherit what we have now? Watch Emma become a midwife in a town without mothers left to attend. Watch Thomas learn a trade no one can afford to pay for?"

Matthew shifted by the door, forgotten until his voice broke the tension. "My pa says the same, sir. About there being nothing left here for us young ones." He ducked his head when both men turned to look at him. "Says that's why he sold our cow for wagon money last week."

William's hand tightened on his walking stick. "Matthew, tell Mrs. Wheeler I'll be home once the storm passes." His eyes never left Caleb's face. "After I've shown my son something."

Matthew slipped out of the shop and into the rain, leaving the door to bang shut behind him. William crossed to the workshop's back wall, where decades of family history still hung beneath dust covers. He pulled the cloth from one shelf, revealing Caleb's childhood carvings—crude attempts at horses and wagons, each carefully preserved.

"Remember this one?" William lifted a miniature wooden horse, its legs uneven, its neck too long. "First piece you ever finished alone. Said you had to get it right because Thomas Cooper's father had ordered a whole set for his store window."

"I was eight," Caleb said quietly. "Cooper paid me two pennies for it."

"Paid you its worth because that's what honest craft meant then. What it still means here." William set the horse down among the packed crates. "Out there?" He gestured toward the door. "Out there, they say a man can claim three hundred and twenty acres just for arriving. What's craft worth in a place like that?"

"Sarah's carrying another," Caleb said, his voice low. "We think... we're almost certain."

William paused as he held the carved horse. "Does your mother know?"

"No one knows. Not yet. Not until Sarah's sure." Caleb reached for James's cradle. "But if we are... if there is... I won't have another child born into a dying town. I won't watch another fever season wondering if-"

"And you think the trail's safer?" William's voice carried no judgment now. "Think a child born in a wagon bed, two thousand miles from proper doctors-"

"A child born free of mortgages, bank failures, and half-price work might have a chance at something better." Caleb straightened despite his leg's protest. "Emma, Thomas, and Margaret deserve more than watching their father's craft die by inches."

The storm's fury began to fade, leaving only the steady drumming of rain on the roof. William stood silent, the carved horse still in his weathered hands, looking at his son as if seeing him for the first time.

"Your mother's got letters," he said finally. "From women who watched the trail take everything they loved. She'll want you to read them. She'd want Sarah to understand what she's asking of her grandchildren."

"I'll read them," Caleb promised. "We'll all read them. But Father..." He gestured to the workshop's walls, empty ledgers, and half-packed crates. "We're already losing everything we love. Might as well lose it trying for something better."

William set the horse down among the wrapped tools. Its uneven legs made it tilt, the way Caleb's first attempts at joinery had always tilted. "You're a better carpenter than I ever was," he said quietly. "Better father, too, probably. But son..." He turned toward the door. "Some dreams cost more than a man can afford to pay."

By afternoon, the storm had settled into steady rain when Sarah Wheeler collapsed in the market square. One moment, she stood examining Williams's remaining stock of dried herbs; the next, her knees buckled, sending bottles scattering across rain-slicked boards.

Caleb saw it happen through the workshop window—Catherine Barrett caught her daughter before she hit the ground, and Emma's small figure darted from behind Morrison's empty storefront. In his haste to reach them, his leg nearly gave out, and pain shot from hip to ankle.

"Get her to my cottage," Catherine ordered, "Emma, run. Tell your father-"

"I'm here." Caleb reached for her, but Catherine pushed him aside.

"Not here," she said quietly.

They helped Sarah to Catherine's cottage.

Sarah's face was pale white. "Mother, I don't need-"

"You need to be sure," Catherine interrupted.

Caleb's hands tightened on his walking stick. "Sarah?"

"I thought..." She paused. "I was almost certain, but then today..."

"The symptoms?" Catherine's tone shifted to professional inquiry, though her hands shook slightly as she paged through her journal.

"Like with James, at first. Morning sickness. Dizziness. But then..." Sarah's eyes found Emma still hovering by the herb shelf. "Emma, go help your brother with his lessons."

"When was your last monthly? Is there any bleeding? Is the pain different from James's time?" Catherine asked as she examined her daughter.

Sarah answered softly to each question.

"Not with child," Catherine announced finally. "Just exhaustion."

"You're certain?" Sarah asked.

"Certain as I can be."

Caleb shifted his weight. "Sarah, if you're not certain about this-"

"I'm certain about what's happening to Williamsport," she replied, standing carefully from the birthing chair. "Certain about what staying means for our children." She placed her hand on Emma's shoulder. "Certain about watching our daughter learn a trade that's dying with the town."

Catherine's fingers gripped her journal's worn cover. "Better a dying trade than a dead daughter," she said quietly. "Better empty appointments than empty cradles."

"I lost one child in a proper town with proper doctors," Sarah said, her voice steady now. "Lost him with every remedy within reach, with my mother's knowledge at hand." She touched the birthing chair's smooth arm. "The fever didn't care about our careful preparations then. Won't care about them next time, whether we stay or go."

"Your father brought warnings today," Sarah said quietly to Caleb. "Didn't he?"

Caleb nodded. "About the trail. About risks."

"And James?" Her voice cracked.

"And James."

"We should head back," Caleb said, watching the light fade. "Thomas will be waiting with his lessons, and Margaret–"

"Margaret needs watching in this weather," Sarah finished. "Last rain brought her fever."

As they stepped outside, the rain had softened to mist. Catherine stood in her doorway, watching her daughter and granddaughter walk away in the muddy street.

"Sarah," she called after them. "The journey west... it's not just about what you might lose." She paused, "It's about what you've already lost by staying."

The night wrapped around the Wheeler house like a winter quilt, heavy with rain. "Your father's right about one thing," Sarah said, barely carrying over the thunder. "The leg won't thank you for two thousand miles of prairie."

"The leg doesn't thank me for Lancashire oak or Harrison's half-price," Caleb replied. "Doesn't thank me for watching our children wear patched clothes while the bank holds our mortgage."

"William offered us the farm." Sarah's chair scraped against the kitchen floor. "Good land already worked. A proper house for the children."

"His house. His land. His rules about how to work it. Watch Thomas learn to farm instead of build. Watch Emma give up her books for butter churning?"

Thunder cracked closer, making the house timbers groan. Lightning illuminated the workshop's silhouette through the window, its closing notice still hanging limply. Emma crouched on the stairs and counted seconds between flash and sound, the way Thomas had taught her to measure storm distance.

"Mother thinks I'm with child," Sarah said suddenly. "Thought I was, anyway, until today."

"Are you..." Caleb's voice caught. "Was she certain about-"

"Not with child," Sarah answered quickly. "Just tired. Worried. Seeing signs in shadows because... Because part of me wanted it to be true. Wanted something new to believe in."

Caleb's leg must have been caught wrong as he moved - something crashed, and a chair toppled. Emma bit back a gasp, pressing herself smaller against the stairs. Below, her father's breath came sharp with pain.

"Signs in shadows," he repeated, voice rough. "Like William's newspaper clippings? Like Martha's letters about women who never came home?"

Sarah's steps moved across the kitchen, probably to help him up. "Like James's fever coming back every time Margaret sneezes. Thomas's cough makes us both wake up at night. Like-"

"Like watching the town die around us?" The chair scraped again as Caleb righted it. "Like counting Harrison's promises against Cooper's closed doors?"

Emma was catching every word. She'd filled three notebooks since winter - since the first whispers of Oregon had started filtering through Williamsport's streets. Each page carried pieces of their family's choice.

Sarah's voice dropped lower, making Emma strain to hear. "She gave me my grandmother's journal—the one from the crossing from England. Three babies were born on that ship. Two survived. One..." Another pause. "One buried at sea, with nothing but a canvas for a cradle."

"Sarah-"

"But three more were born in Pennsylvania once they landed. Three more because they dared to leave what was known." Sarah's voice strengthened. "Including my grandmother. Including the woman who taught my mother everything she knows about bringing life into the world."

Lightning flashed again, catching Emma's pencil mid-word. In that brief illumination, she saw her mother standing at the kitchen window, Catherine's journal clutched against her chest. Caleb leaned on the overturned chair, his right leg held carefully, the way it always was after rain.

"Your father failed his journey west," Sarah said quietly. "Did he tell you that today? Along with his warnings?"

"To Ohio," Caleb confirmed. "Year before I was born."

"And came back to his father's workshop, his father's tools, his father's way of doing things." Sarah's voice carried no judgment, only understanding. "Like he wants you to come back to his farm, his land, his-"

"His safety," Caleb finished. "His certainty about what a Wheeler ought to be."

"I dream about James," Sarah said finally. "Not about the fever - about what he might have been. A carpenter like his father, maybe. Or something else entirely, something Oregon might have shown him how to be."

The chair creaked as Caleb shifted. "Sarah, if you're not certain about this... if today's scare made you think twice..."

"Today made me think about Margaret," Sarah interrupted. "About how she plays in your wood shavings without fear, even after James. About how she sees wagons pass and dreams about sleeping under the stars instead of worrying about what we're leaving behind."

"And Emma?" Caleb asked. "Watching everything, writing everything down? Drawing Oregon maps on her slate instead of her sums?"

"Emma understands more than we want her to," Sarah answered. "Like she understood about James before we told her. Like she understands about the workshop closing, about what it means that Cooper's gone and Williams sold his store."

"My father thinks I'm running away," Caleb said with a rough voice. "From the workshop's legacy, from Wheeler tradition, from..." He paused, "From James's ghost."

Sarah's steps crossed the kitchen again, boards creaking under her feet. "Maybe we are running," she said quietly. "From fever seasons and empty cradles and children wearing patches while the bank holds our future." The sound of Catherine's journal on the table punctuated her words. "But James taught us about running, didn't he? You can run as far as Philadelphia with its proper doctors and still not outrun what's coming."

"Cooper asked me something," Caleb said, "before he closed his store. He asked if I remembered building his counter with maple inlay, which took two months to finish. He said he'd thought his boy would stand behind that counter someday, the same as he had and his father had."

"And now?"

"Now his boy's learning to read trail maps instead of ledger books. Learning to pack wagon beds instead of store shelves." The chair creaked again as Caleb shifted. "Same as Thomas is learning knots instead of joints, same as Emma's studying herbs instead of figures."

Lightning flashed again, closer now. Emma caught glimpses of her parents' faces - her mother still at the window, her father gripping the chair's back with whitened knuckles.

"I keep thinking," Sarah said softly, "about what Mother said. About it not being just what we might lose by going." She turned from the window. "James is already lost, Caleb. The workshop's already closing. The town's already dying around us."

"Father would say that's why we should stay. Help rebuild. Keep the tradition alive."

"Tradition?" Sarah's scoffed. "Like the tradition of Wheeler woodcraft? When was the last time someone paid full price for your work? When was the last time an apprentice came asking to learn?"

"The children deserve better than watching their father's craft die," Sarah continued. "Better than learning trades no one can afford to pay for. Better than-" She stopped suddenly. "Emma Wheeler, if you're going to listen on the stairs, you might as well come down and write where you can see properly."

The pencil dropped from Emma's startled fingers, clattering down the wooden steps. She heard her father's sharp intake of breath and her mother's quiet sigh. Lamplight spilled up the staircase, showing her hunched figure now.

"How long have you been there?" Caleb asked though they all knew the answer.

Emma descended the last few stairs. "Since the storm got bad," she admitted. "I was... I wanted to understand."

Morning came gray and sullen, the storm's remnants still dripping from Williamsport's eaves. Thomas stood in the empty mercantile storage yard, his wooden sword trailing patterns in puddles that reflected the lead-colored sky. Since Cooper closed, the yard had become his practice ground—a place to scout, track, and prepare.

"Look who it is," a voice bellowed from behind the crates. "The Oregon fever victim."

William Harrison Jr. emerged behind the stacked wood, followed by the Cooper boy and young Timothy Brooks. All sons of proper Williamsport families wore boots that hadn't yet needed patching.

"Pa says your family's running away," Harrison continued, moving to block Thomas's path to the yard's exit. "Says your father's too proud to accept proper help from his kin."

Thomas's grip tightened on his wooden sword. He'd carved it himself, using scraps from his father's workshop.

"We're not running," he said, his missing front tooth making the words whistle slightly. "We're going to build something new."

Harrison's laugh echoed off the empty storage shed. "Build something? Pa tells it that your father can't even build proper furniture anymore. Not with that bad leg. Not with-"

"My father builds better than anyone," Thomas said, feeling the heat rise in his cheeks. "Better than your father's cheap pine desk that wobbles when he writes his worthless bank notes."

The first punch surprised Thomas, Harrison's fist connecting with his jaw hard enough to send him stumbling back into a rain puddle. Cold water soaked through his trousers as Cooper's boy moved to block one escape route, Brooks the other.

"Take it back," Harrison demanded, standing over him. "About my father's desk. About the bank notes."

Thomas tasted blood where his loose tooth had finally given up its hold.

"Truth hurts worse than fists," he said, using one of his mother's sayings. "Oregon fever hurts less than watching your town die around you."

This time, he was ready for Harrison's swing. The wooden sword came up like his father had shown him - not to hit, but to block, to defend. The impact jarred his arms, but he held firm.

"Your father's a coward," Harrison spat, nursing his knuckles where they'd struck hard oak. "Running west because he can't compete with Millvale's prices. Because he's too crippled to."

Thomas didn't remember moving. One moment, he stood in the puddle; the next, his wooden sword lay forgotten as his fists found Harrison's pristine shirt front. They went down together in the mud, rolling between empty packing crates while Cooper and Brooks shouted encouragement to Harrison.

Pain exploded across Thomas's nose as Harrison's elbow caught him wrong. But his smaller size worked to his advantage in the narrow space between crates, letting him slip free of the older boy's grasp. His father had taught him about leverage - how even small forces, properly applied, could move great weights.

"Fight like a man," Harrison taunted, trying to corner him against the shed wall.

Thomas drove forward, ducking under Harrison's guard, his shoulder catching the older boy's stomach, driving them back into a stack of empty barrels. The crash brought shouts from the street beyond the yard.

"William Harrison Junior!" The banker's voice cut through the morning mist. "What in God's name are you doing?"

But it wasn't Harrison Sr. who reached them first. Caleb's uneven steps splashed through puddles, his bad leg dragging slightly in haste. Thomas felt his father's strong hands pull him up from the mud.

"He insulted you," Thomas managed through bleeding lips. He said you were running because you couldn't compete with Millvale."

Caleb's fingers felt Thomas's face. Through his one eye that wasn't swelling shut, Thomas saw something flash across his father's expression - pride warring with worry, anger with understanding.

"Fighting won't change their minds, son," he said quietly. Then, louder as Harrison Sr. approached: "Though some minds seem set on misunderstanding, no matter what's said."

The banker pulled his son up roughly, taking in the torn clothes and muddy boots. "Wheeler," he said, nodding stiffly. "Your boy seems to have inherited more than just your craft."

"Seems he has," Caleb agreed, his hand steady on Thomas's shoulder. "Including a taste for truth, however bitter it comes."

More townspeople had gathered, drawn by the noise. Thomas saw Emma's face in the workshop window across the street, her notebook probably already recording this new chapter in their family's story. Cooper's father stood in his empty store's doorway, watching his son slink away from the battle scene.

"Truth?" Harrison Sr. straightened his son's collar. "Truth is, Wheeler, you're spreading this Oregon fever through decent families. Making working folks think they're too good for honest labor at fair prices."

"Fair prices?" Caleb's laugh held the same edge Thomas had heard in his voice during midnight arguments. "Like Katherine's chest? Like the mortgages your bank held before Philadelphia called them due?"

Thomas felt his father's hand tighten on his shoulder. Through the swelling around his eye, he saw William Wheeler appear at the crowd's edge, his walking stick marking time on wet cobblestones.

"The boy needs discipline," Harrison Sr. said, steering his son toward the street. "Something lacking in families caught up in Western fantasies."

"The boy needs hope," Caleb replied, loud enough for the gathering crowd to hear. "Something is lacking in towns where bank notes are worth more than honest craft."

William's steps brought him closer, drawing attention like a lodestone draws iron filings. "Grandson," he said, looking at Thomas's bloodied face. Your grandmother has willow bark tea brewing. You'd best come to get some before that eye swells wholly shut."

Caleb's hand remained steady on Thomas's shoulder as they turned toward home. The wooden sword lay forgotten in the mud, its oak grain darkened by rain and blood. Thomas took a step toward it, but his father's grip tightened.

"Leave it," Caleb said softly. "Real scouts carry different weapons. Patience. Knowledge. Understanding of what's worth fighting for."

They moved through Williamsport's morning streets, past Cooper's empty store and Williams's boarded windows. Thomas's eye throbbed in time with his father's limping steps.

"Did you fight?" he asked suddenly, looking up at his father. "When you were my age?"

"Once," Caleb admitted. "When Bobby Thompson said my father's joints weren't true. That Millvale work was better, even then." His lips quirked slightly. "Your grandfather had willow bark tea waiting that day, too."

William's walking stick marked their pace from behind, its rhythm steady as wagon wheels on rutted roads.

"The tea helps," he said, "But understanding helps more—understanding what's worth bloodied knuckles and what's better left to time's judgment."

They reached the workshop door, where Emma waited, her notebook clutched tight. Sarah appeared beside her, already gathering herbs for bandages. Her midwife's skills turned to this minor crisis.

"Harrison's boy?" she asked, though they knew the answer. "About Oregon?"

"About Pa," Thomas corrected, wincing as she found tender spots. "About his leg, and the workshop, and-"

"And things that don't matter halfway to Independence," Caleb finished. His leg had begun trembling from the morning's quick response to the fight. "Things that won't mean anything once we've crossed the Mississippi."

William stood in the workshop doorway, watching Sarah tend his grandson's wounds. His eyes moved to the half-packed crates, the wrapped tools, and the canvas-shrouded cradle still holding so many memories.

"Some things follow," he said quietly. "Some weights can't be left behind, no matter how far west you travel."

But Thomas, through his one good eye, saw something else in his grandfather's face that looked almost like pride. The same look he'd seen in his father's eyes when the fight broke out.

"Did you win?" Emma whispered as Sarah turned to fetch more herbs. "Against Harrison?"

Thomas touched his swollen eye, feeling the price of standing ground before leaving it. "Depends," he answered, "on what winning means."

The evening gathered early, pushed by clouds still heavy with unshed rain. This time, William returned to the workshop carrying more than his walking stick – the family Bible tucked under one arm, Martha at his side with James's baptismal gown folded over her hands like a peace offering.

Caleb looked up from the crate he was packing. Thomas sat nearby, his eye darkened to purple, carefully wrapping his grandfather's teaching tools in a clean cloth.

"Your mother thought it was time," William said, setting the Bible on the workbench. Its brass clasps reflected in the light. "Time to speak of inheritance and legacy."

Martha moved to where Sarah stood amid half-packed belongings, the baptismal gown passing between them. Emma appeared at the workshop door, drawn by the tone in her grandfather's voice. Even Margaret, usually asleep by this hour, watched from her nest of wood shavings in the corner.

"Four generations of Wheelers," William began, opening the Bible to its family pages. "Four generations working wood in this shop, building things that lasted." His finger passed over names and dates, each one written in careful script. "Your great-grandfather carved this bench we're sitting on. Your grandfather built the cradle that held you, that held your son-"

"And now you want us to stay," Caleb said quietly. "Take the farm, keep the tradition, and let Thomas learn to plow instead of learning to plane."

"I want you to understand what you're leaving," William corrected. "What can't be packed in wagons or measured in acres." He turned another page, where births had given way to marriages, marriages to deaths. "Your great-grandmother helped birth half the town's children. Your mother's gardens fed families through winter famines. This shop..." He gestured to walls that had witnessed sixty years of craft. "This shop built their cradles, their coffins, their hope for something solid in uncertain times."

Sarah slowly stroked the delicate embroidery on the baptismal gown. "And now uncertain times are calling us west," she said softly. "Like they called your parents here from England, William. Like they called Martha's family from Lancaster County."

"That was different," William started, but Martha's hand on his arm stopped him.

"Was it?" she asked, her voice gentle but firm. We carry our traditions with us. We have them in our hands and hearts, and how we teach our children to face what comes." She looked at Thomas's bruised face, Emma's ever-present notebook, and Margaret playing quietly with wood scraps. "Even if what comes means leaving everything familiar behind."

Caleb's leg gave out suddenly, forcing him to sit on his father's workbench—the same bench where he'd learned to read grain, test joints, and build things that would outlast their maker. William watched him settle and saw the pain flash across his face before being hidden away.

"The farm's good land," William said, his voice softer now. "Three hundred acres, clear-titled. No banknotes, no mortgages. Room for two families to grow, to build, to"

"To watch our children inherit what's dying?" Caleb interrupted. "Watch Emma learn accounts for empty ledgers? Watch Thomas master tools no one can afford to pay for?"

"Your grandfather's tools," William continued, gesturing to the wrapped bundles Thomas had been packing. "English steel, brought across an ocean because he believed American timber deserved the finest craftsmanship. He meant them for your children, Caleb. Meant them to stay in Wheeler's hands."

"And they will," Caleb replied. "They'll build homes in Oregon timber, cradles for Oregon children, benches for Oregon churches." His hand found a wrapped plane - his grandfather's favorite, the one that had taught him how to read wood's voice. "They'll carry Wheeler craft west, where honest work still means something."

Martha stepped forward, still holding the baptismal gown. "James wore this," she said quietly. "For his three days of health. For his three days of hope." Her fingers smoothed invisible wrinkles from the delicate fabric. "I wrapped him in it again at the end. When fever took what all our traditions couldn't save."

"The fever took him here," Martha continued, looking at her son. "In a proper town, with proper doctors. With his grandmother's remedies, his mother's care, and all the certainty we thought would protect him." She held the gown out to Sarah. "Perhaps... perhaps certainty isn't what our children need most."

William's hand tightened on his walking stick. "Martha-"

"No, Listen." She turned to face him fully. "You taught our son to build things that last. But you also taught him to measure true, to know when wood's too weak for what's asked of it." Her eyes found the empty ledgers, the half-price notice on Harrison's chest, the wrapped tools waiting for whatever came next. "Perhaps he's measuring truer than we want to see."

"Your mother," William said slowly, "saw Oregon in you before I did. I saw it the day Harrison first offered half-price for Katherine's chest. She said you had the same look she remembered from my eyes that year before you were born."

Caleb's hands gripped his grandfather's plane. "The year you tried for Ohio?"

"The year I was too proud to admit failure until we'd lost everything but our lives. Came crawling back to my father's workshop, took his charity, and lived under his rules because I was too scared to try again."

Martha moved to stand behind her husband, one hand finding his shoulder. "Tell him the rest, William. Tell him what you've never told anyone but me."

"I see them sometimes," William said, his voice rough as unsanded oak. "In my dreams. The children we might have had out there. The life we might have built if I'd been braver and tried again instead of settling for safe harbor." He looked at his son. "See them in Thomas's adventures, in Emma's questions, in Margaret's way of looking west like she already knows what's waiting."

Sarah cradled the baptismal gown, its whiteness stark against her dark apron. "William—"

"Let me finish," he cut in. "I need to say this while I have the courage." His hand found Martha's on his shoulder. "When James... when the fever took him... I thought it was a sign. Thought it meant Wheeler blood was meant for Pennsylvania soil, that trying to leave would only bring more grief."

"But today," William continued, "watching my grandson stand his ground before leaving it... watching him defend his father's choice with bloodied knuckles and blackened eyes..." He stopped, swallowing hard. "Made me remember something my father told me when I came back from Ohio with my dreams in tatters."

"What did he say?" Caleb asked quietly.

"Sometimes a man has to lose everything he has to find everything he could be." William's fingers touched the Bible's brass clasps. "Said he'd rather see me fail trying for something better than succeed at something safe."

Martha's hands moved to the Bible, gently closing its family history pages. "We didn't come here tonight to offer the farm again," she said softly, " though William needed to offer it one last time for his peace." She lifted something else from beside the workbench—a wrapped bundle they hadn't noticed her carrying in. "We came to give you these."

The cloth fell away, revealing tools older than the workshop itself—William's father's tools, brought from England.

"They belong in Wheeler's hands," William said gruffly. "Always have. Always will." He lifted a plane that bore his father's initials, worn smooth by generations of callused palms. "But maybe... maybe they belong in hands brave enough to shape new timber, not just tend what's already been worked."

Caleb's leg trembled as he stood. These weren't just tools—they were permission, a blessing, and a release from the guilt of leaving.

"The farm will wait," William continued. "If Oregon proves false, if the trail proves too hard, if..." He stopped, then forced himself to finish. "If you find you need safe harbor again. But son..." His hand found Caleb's shoulder. "Don't come back because you're afraid to fail. Come back only if you've failed trying for something better."

Sarah stepped forward, still holding James's baptismal gown. "And this?" she asked softly. "What do we do with this?"

Martha touched the delicate fabric one last time. "Take it," she said. "Take it west. Let it remind you that some things are worth the risk of loss." Her eyes found Emma's notebook, Thomas's bruised face, and Margaret's quiet watching from her corner. "That everything precious carries the price of possible grief."

"Your grandfather," William said suddenly, "told me something else when I returned from Ohio. Something I was too ashamed then to understand." He lifted the walking stick that had marked his steps for decades. "Said a man needs solid ground to stand on, but he needs the courage to leave it more."

The stick passed from father to son, generations of Wheeler's hands marked in its smooth wood. Caleb gripped it, feeling the weight of legacy and permission in equal measure.

"Thomas," William called. "Bring those tools you were wrapping. Time you learned their proper names, their proper use." He looked at his son. "Time you learned them from your father, the way he learned them from me, the way I learned them from mine."

"Pa?" Margaret's small voice came from her corner. "Can I build, too?"

The workshop was filled with unexpected laughter—William's deep chuckle, Martha's gentle mirth, Sarah's relief spilling over into joy. Even Thomas managed a grin despite his swollen face.

"Yes, little one," Caleb said, reaching for his grandfather's tools with one hand and his father's walking stick with the other. "We'll all build something new."

Dawn broke over the Williamsport cemetery with a thick, low-hanging fog. The Wheeler family moved between graves still wet with spring dew, Sarah carrying her mother's herbs, Caleb leaning on his father's walking stick. They came to stand before the smallest stone, its surface yet to weather a full year of seasons.

JAMES WHEELER

Beloved Son

Six Days of Grace

God's Will Be Done

Emma clutched her notebook, but for once, her pencil was still. Some moments she was learning couldn't be captured in words. Thomas held his carved wooden horse - the last thing he'd shown his baby brother before the fever took hold. Margaret followed in their wake, trailing wood shavings from her apron pockets like bread crumbs in a fairy tale.

Sarah knelt first, her skirt gathering dew from the grass. The herbs in her hands were the same ones that had failed to save James—yarrow, feverfew, willow bark—but now they served a different purpose. She began planting them around his stone, each pressed into the soil holding her son.

"So he'll know," she said softly, working them into the soil. "Know we're not leaving him alone."

Caleb's grip tightened on the walking stick. The stone seemed smaller somehow than when they'd first placed it—like James himself, brief as morning mist, gone before they'd learned his face correctly.

Emma stepped forward, Bible clutched in her free hand. She'd marked the passages herself, choosing words of journey, faith, and hope in unseen things. Her voice carried clear in the cemetery quiet:

"'By faith Abraham, when called to go to a place he would later receive as his inheritance, obeyed and went, even though he did not know where he was going.'"

Thomas moved next, setting his carved horse at the stone's base. He'd worked on it secretly since the decision to leave, whittling between lessons and chores.

"For watching over us," he whispered, touching the stone's cold surface. "While we're gone."

Margaret's wood shavings fell like scattered blessings, curling in the damp air before settling around Sarah's planted herbs. The child seemed to understand the moment; her usually restless energy held still.

"Your grandmother fought me," Sarah said, her fingers still working soil around the herbs. When we named you James, she said it was tempting fate, giving you a name that carried so much Wheeler history." Now I wonder if we tempted fate by holding too tight to what was known instead of looking toward what could be."

Caleb shifted his weight, the walking stick sinking slightly into the soft ground. "He should have been the one to carry our craft forward, to build something new from old skills."

"And so he will." Sarah's voice carried surprising strength. "Through them." She nodded toward their living children—Emma with careful notes, Thomas with his brave heart, Margaret with her innocent wisdom—" through whatever they build in Oregon's timber."

Emma's Bible pages rustled as she found another passage: "'For we know that if our earthly house of this tabernacle were dissolved, we have a building of God, a house not made with hands, eternal in the heavens.'"

Thomas knelt beside his mother, adding a smooth riverstone to his wooden horse. He'd been collecting them since winter, each chosen for its perfect shape. "For finding the trail," he explained when they all looked at him. "So he can follow if he wants to."

Margaret moved to the stone's other side, opposite Sarah's plantings. She pulled not just shavings from her apron but something more – a tiny wood block carved with unpracticed hands.

"House," she said solemnly, setting it beside Thomas's horse. "For James."

The fog began to lift, and the morning sun broke through.

4

CROSSING THE THRESHOLD

Independence, Missouri – April 1843

The wagon wheels sank deep into Independence's muddy streets as Caleb guided their team through the morning market crowd. Wagons pressed in from all sides, their canvas covers brilliant white against the spring sky. His right leg ached from working the brake, but he suppressed his expressions as much as possible.

"Pa!" Thomas called from the back. "I counted forty-seven wagons just in the square!"

"Forty-eight," Emma corrected as she diligently recorded everything – the press of people, the shouts of traders, the rich smell of coffee from the hotel's open windows.

Caleb shifted his grip on the reins as a fancy carriage cut across their path, nearly clipping their lead horse. The delay gave him time to study the crowd – farmers with callused hands like his own, merchants in city clothes, and Cherokee traders watching the chaos near the market's edge.

A man stood in the doorway of the trading post, his attention fixed on their approaching wagon. "The iron's wearing thin on that back wheel," the man called as they drew closer. It won't last past Council Bluffs." He stepped forward, revealing hands crossed with the scars of experience. Samuel Cooper. And you'll be needing my help."

Before Caleb could respond, their wheel caught in a deep rut. Sarah grabbed his arm as the wagon tilted dangerously. Margaret buried her face in her mother's shawl while Thomas whooped with excitement.

"Steady now," Cooper said, already moving to brace the wheel. His sure movements spoke of countless similar rescues. "Let's get you folks clear of this mess before that wheel gives out entirely."

The trading post's weathered sign creaked overhead as Cooper guided them to a sideyard already crowded with wagons in various states of repair. Each bore the marks of long travel yet to come—reinforced axles, double canvas, and water barrels strapped tight.

"Pennsylvania?" Cooper asked though something in his tone suggested he already knew.

Caleb nodded, climbing down carefully to examine the wheel. "Wheeler family. I'm a carpenter by trade."

"Are you now?" Cooper's interest sharpened. He gestured to Caleb's toolbox, strapped carefully atop their load. "Mind if I see your work?"

Sarah caught Caleb's eye as she helped Margaret down. They'd agreed to be cautious with strangers, but something about Cooper's direct manner invited trust. Caleb retrieved his prized plane.

Cooper whistled softly as he tested the blade. "Fine work. You do your smithing on this?"

"My grandfather's work," Caleb replied. "Been in the family five generations."

"And now it's heading to Oregon." Cooper handed back the plane with careful respect. "You'll want to wrap that in oilcloth. Trail dust can dull a blade quicker than cheap steel."

Emma had already discovered the maps covering Cooper's trading post walls. Her finger traced the long curve of the Platte River while Thomas pressed his nose against a glass case containing Native American arrowheads.

"First rule of the trail," Cooper said, watching them. "Everything serves two purposes, or it stays behind." He turned back to Caleb. "Which brings us to that auction notice in your wagon."

The auction handbill was face-down, but Cooper noticed.

"Tomorrow morning," Caleb confirmed.

Cooper nodded slowly. "Second rule of the trail – what you leave behind makes room for what you'll become. Now, let's consider keeping your family rolling long enough to find out what that might be."

The auction house before them had dark windows despite the morning sun. Caleb's hands tightened on his grandfather's corner cabinet as he and Cooper maneuvered it through the narrow doorway. Each scrape of wood against wood felt like a personal wound.

"Be careful with that piece," Sarah called from the wagon. She stood amid their dismantled life, wrapping her grandmother's China in quilts she'd sewn from scraps of unused fabric. Her movements were quick but gentle, as if trying to cushion the plates and the memories they represented.

Emma followed behind them, her journal open despite the awkward angle. "Pine with cherry inlay," she wrote, "carved by Great-Grandfather Wheeler for his daughter's wedding. Summer, 1789." Her small hand pressed against the cabinet's side, feeling the generations of polish.

"Got the inventory list here," the auctioneer called, his voice echoing through the cavernous room. "Need everything labeled and arranged by noon." He barely glanced at the cabinet. "Furniture in the back. Tools by the window for better light."

Caleb set the cabinet down more roughly than he'd intended. The auctioneer's dismissal of his grandfather's craftsmanship struck harder than he'd expected.

"Pa?" Thomas appeared at his elbow, clutching his wooden toy chest. "Do we have to sell everything?"

The chest was Caleb's first project with Thomas, built on quiet Sunday afternoons. Each joint represented a lesson in patience, and each smoothed edge represented a small victory. Thomas's fingers traced the carved horses on the lid as if memorizing their shape.

"Not everything," Caleb answered, though the list of what they could keep grew shorter with each calculation. "Just what we can't carry."

"But it's mine," Thomas whispered. "I helped make it."

Before Caleb could respond, a sharp cry from the wagon drew his attention. Margaret had discovered her favorite wooden horse missing from its hiding place in Sarah's sewing basket.

"I told you she'd find it," Emma said, already moving to comfort her sister. She had that same look she'd worn when baby James died – too old for her ten years.

Sarah descended from the wagon, her arms full of wrapped China. A single teacup slipped free, shattering on the wooden floor. The sound startled them all.

"Leave it," she said when Emma moved to help. "It's just... it's just a thing."

But her voice cracked as she spoke, and Caleb saw her fingers press against the quilt. Each piece was wrapped in memories – Sunday dinners, Christmas mornings, the last meal they'd shared with James.

Cooper appeared in the doorway. "I've got room in the storehouse if you need a moment to sort things properly." He gestured to the growing crowd outside. "Early buyers are already gathering."

Caleb arranged the tools he was prepared to sell and set aside a few he could justify keeping.

Thomas sat with his toy chest, methodically removing each treasure – smooth stones from the creek behind their workshop, a carved whistle Caleb had made him last Christmas, the arrowhead he'd found in Grandfather's field. The chest grew emptier while his pockets grew fuller.

Sarah finally rewrapped the China. "We should finish before the crowd grows larger."

Caleb nodded, gathering his remaining tools. As he turned to leave, he paused and looked back. "Pa?" Emma stood in the doorway, clutching her journal tight. "I've got it all written down—every piece, every story."

He touched her shoulder gently. "That's worth more than any cabinet, Emma girl."

The auctioneer bellowed as he organized his assistants for the sale. Sarah straightened her apron, squaring her shoulders like before difficult births. Margaret clung to her skirts while Thomas kept one hand in his pocket as if protecting his hidden keepsakes.

"Time to go," Caleb said quietly. But as they stepped into the street, he couldn't help wondering if Oregon's promises were worth the price they'd already begun to pay.

The auctioneer's voice carried across the yard as Caleb helped arrange the last pieces. Sarah had disappeared around the back of the auction house, claiming she needed to check Margaret's bonnet strings. But when he found her, she stood alone, one hand bracing against the shop, shoulders shaking silently.

"It's a hard thing, that first letting go." The voice came from behind them, warm with understanding. A woman approached, her calico dress faded but well-mended, her face weathered by sun and wind. "Rebecca Mills. And you'd be the Wheelers that Samuel Cooper mentioned."

Sarah quickly wiped her eyes, but Rebecca waved away the gesture. "I cried for three days straight when we sold Mother's dresser. Real mahogany, brought from Boston." She settled on an empty crate, patting the space beside her. "That was two years ago, before our first attempt at the trail."

"First attempt?" Sarah asked as she sat beside her.

"Turned back at Fort Laramie that year. Snow came early." Rebecca's voice held no shame in the admission. "Learned more from failing than we might have from an easy success. Taught me which memories weigh more than their worth and which travel light."

From inside came the sharp crack of the auctioneer's gavel. Sarah flinched at each fall as if the sound struck her directly. They could hear Emma's careful voice reading descriptions of each piece through the wall – clear and steady.

"Your girl's got a good head," Rebecca observed. "Been watching her all morning, making her lists and drawings. She'll need that eye for detail on the trail." She reached into her apron pocket and withdrew a small leather pouch. "Speaking of useful things – brought you some starting plants. Feverfew, yarrow, shepherd's purse. I hear you're a midwife?"

Sarah's hands moved automatically to accept the pouch, her fingers identifying each dried bundle by touch. "Was a midwife," she corrected softly. "Here, at least."

"Trail needs healers more than any town," Rebecca replied. "Last summer, I watched a Cheyenne woman stop bleeding with plants I'd walked past a hundred times. She showed me how to find them, how to use them right. Knowledge weighs nothing in your wagon but could save a life."

Emma appeared around the corner. She hesitated at seeing the stranger, but something in Rebecca's worn smile drew her closer.

"I heard you talking about plants," she said, pulling out her journal. "Could I write down what you learned from the Cheyenne woman?"

Rebecca's eyes crinkled with approval. "Smart girl. Brought my notes if you'd like to copy them." She produced a small, dog-eared notebook. "Two years of trail medicine, written plain as I could make it."

The sound of boyish laughter drew their attention. Thomas had discovered Rebecca's son James practicing with a small knife, carefully carving a piece of kindling. The boys had already fallen into that easy friendship of the young, heads bent together over their task.

"James can show him the proper grip," Rebecca offered, seeing Sarah's worried look. "Boy needs to know his way around a blade before we reach the Platte."

Margaret came around the corner, crying softly. Caleb realized that her fist was wrapped around something small and wooden – one of the pegs from her father's workbench. The bench itself must have just sold.

The auctioneer's voice rose again, announcing the corner cabinet sale. Sarah's hands tightened on the leather pouch of herbs, but her voice remained steady. "Tell me more about the plants you learned. The ones for bleeding, especially."

Emma wrote as Rebecca began her lesson. Thomas and James tested knife grips against kindling, their laughter mixing with the auctioneer's calls. Margaret cradled her doll, whispering secrets to it.

Caleb watched them all from the corner of the auction house, noting how Sarah's shoulders had straightened and Emma's questions had grown more confident. Rebecca's presence had shifted something—turned their loss into learning.

Inside, his father's workbench sold for a quarter of its worth. But out here, his family was already building something new.

Cooper's trading post smelled of leather, coffee, and wood smoke. Late afternoon light slanted through dusty windows, catching specks of dust that danced over rows of supplies – iron cookware, coils of rope, stacks of trail guides worn smooth by worried hands.

"First thing you need to understand," Cooper said, spreading a marked map across his counter, "is that everything you think you know about carpentry changes on the trail." His scarred finger traced the route west. "Wood warps differently in the mountain air. Joints that held in Pennsylvania might split when the altitude changes."

Caleb leaned closer, noting the annotations marking water sources, dangerous river crossings, and places where wheels often broke. Each note represented hard-won knowledge.

"Green wood's your enemy out there," Cooper continued. "No time for proper curing. You'll need to learn to read the standing trees and know which ones might give you straight grain in a hurry."

Sarah and Rebecca sorted through medical supplies at the other end of the counter. Emma sat cross-legged on the floor nearby, her journal open, as she copied Cooper's wall map and added Rebecca's notes about where certain medicinal plants could be found.

"The Pawnee know this area," Rebecca said, pointing to a section of Emma's map. "They showed me where the best yarrow grows. Mark that spot – we'll reach it just before the Platte crossing."

Thomas had discovered a collection of Native artifacts displayed behind glass near the front window. He stared through the glass, studying each item closely. Beyond him, through the wavy glass, Caleb could see a group of Cherokee traders arranging their goods in the yard.

"Boy's got good instincts," Cooper observed. "Those men out there know more about survival than any guidebook." He raised his voice slightly. "Thomas? Want to learn how they make those arrows you're admiring?"

Thomas spun around so fast he nearly knocked over a display of tin cups. "Could I?"

"Standing Bear's been trading here fifteen years," Cooper said. "Taught my boy more than I ever could about tracking and survival." He turned back to Caleb. "Which brings us to your wagon. Needs work before it'll carry you to Oregon."

The wagon waited in Cooper's side yard. Other wagons bristled with added supports, extra axles, and reinforced wheels. Their own looked suddenly inadequate, like a riverboat trying to pass for an ocean vessel.

"I can pay-" Caleb began, but Cooper waved him off.

"Your skills are worth more than money out here. Already got three wagons needing repair before the train leaves." He grinned. "Though I wouldn't say no to one of those carved horses the newspaper boy showed off this morning."

Margaret's small voice carried from where she sat with Rebecca's daughter, Mary, learning to fashion a new cornhusk doll. "Like this?" she asked, carefully bending the dried husk.

"Perfect," Mary answered. "Now she needs a dress. Mama says dolls can't go to Oregon in their nightclothes."

Sarah looked up from her medical inventory, catching Caleb's eye. "Rebecca's been teaching me about trail medicine," she said, moving to join him. "Things I never learned from Mother. Plants that grow wild, ways to set bones without proper splints." She hesitated. "Things we might need."

Cooper nodded approvingly. "Knowledge and skills; those are the real currency out here." He turned to his workbench, revealing neat piles of wagon parts and tools.

"Now, let's see what you know about reinforcing axles. Trail's got ways of testing every joint and seam."

For the next hour, Cooper led Caleb through the specifics of trail carpentry—quick repairs, improvised tools, and ways to work around his leg's limitations. Caleb watched Thomas approach the Cherokee traders through the window, attempting a careful bow like he'd seen Cooper give. Standing Bear, a tall man with graying hair, responded by demonstrating how to greet an elder properly.

Sarah worked with Rebecca, learning to identify plants from dried samples and practicing knots for emergency stitching. They shared knowledge accumulated through generations of women keeping families alive.

"Your family adapts quickly," Cooper commented, watching them all. "That's good. Trail changes people faster than distance alone can account for." He handed Caleb a worn leather book. "My trail notes. Copy what you need – you've got the night watches to fill anyway."

"Night watches?"

"Another lesson." Cooper's face grew serious. "Trail's got its own rules and ways of teaching them. Best start learning now."

The auction crowd pressed close in the afternoon heat, their voices echoing off the wooden walls. Caleb stood at the back, his hand tight on his grandfather's plane—one of the few tools he'd justified keeping. Sarah remained outside with Margaret, but Emma insisted on staying.

"Wheeler estate auction," the crier announced, "Fine Pennsylvania craftsmanship, generations of quality." He pointed to the first piece – Sarah's mother's China cabinet. "Starting bid at twenty dollars."

"Fifteen," called a voice from the crowd. Caleb recognized Harrison Senior's profile near the front—a final knife twist.

"Eighteen," countered Mary Blackwell, catching Caleb's eye.

The bidding moved quickly after that. Sarah's China was sold to the hotel owner's wife for half its worth, and the corner cabinet, with its careful inlay and hidden drawers, was sold to a cattle trader who barely glanced at its craftsmanship.

Emma recorded each sale as it was completed: "Mother's China cabinet—$19.50. Grandmother's tea service—$12.75."

"Next item," the crier continued, "Master carpenter's workbench, fifth-generation Wheeler piece..."

Caleb's father's workbench. The one where he'd learned to plane wood straight and true, where he'd taught Emma to mark dovetails, where Thomas had stood on tiptoes to watch him work. Its scarred surface held nineteen years of Wheeler history.

The bidding started low and stayed there. No one wanted a heavy workbench, no matter its provenance. Ultimately, it went to a farmer who mentioned using it for a hay trough.

"Pa?" Emma's voice was barely a whisper. "Should I write down what they will use things for?"

"Just the prices, Emma girl." He didn't want to know how anything would be utilized.

Sarah appeared in the doorway, her face composed but her hands nervously playing with the hem of her apron. Margaret clung to her skirt, clutching her doll. Rebecca Mills stood just behind them.

"Your mother's wedding chest is next," Caleb said softly.

The maple chest gleamed in the afternoon light, its wood rich with decades of careful polishing. Sarah's mother had packed it with quilts and sent her daughter to marry a carpenter who worked wood with love.

The bidding moved too quickly for Emma to follow. When the gavel fell, Rebecca Mills stepped forward to pay.

"Just temporary," she said, touching Sarah's arm. "Until you're settled in Oregon. Some things should stay in the family."

Sarah was unable to maintain her composure. She turned quickly, hugging Rebecca tightly.

Cooper came by near sunset. "Wagon's ready," he said quietly. "Whenever you've seen enough."

The last item was a small table Caleb had made for Sarah when Emma was born. It sold just as dusk fell. The crowd dispersed quickly, eager to collect their purchases before dark.

Harrison Junior shouldered past them, already calling for workers to move his new acquisitions.

"Well," Sarah said into the empty room, her voice steady again. "That's done."

Emma closed her journal with careful deliberation. The final page showed neat columns of figures that added up to less than half what they'd hoped. Barely enough for proper supplies, with nothing left for emergencies.

Rebecca squeezed Sarah's hand. "Come to supper with us. Mary wants to show Margaret more doll-making, and I've got trail bread recipes to share."

"Time to build something new," Cooper said from the doorway. "Something that'll carry you further than any workbench could."

Morning fog clung to Independence's muddy streets as Thomas edged closer to the Cherokee traders' blankets. Standing Bear sat cross-legged before his goods, carefully stringing glass beads. His dark eyes tracked Thomas's approach without seeming to move.

"Remember what I showed you," Cooper called softly from his store doorway. "Respect first."

Thomas attempted the formal bow he'd practiced all evening, nearly overbalancing in his eagerness. Standing Bear's weathered face creased with a slight smile.

"The young one learns quickly," he said to Cooper in English, then turned to Thomas. "But a bow should flow like water, not fall like a stone." He set aside his beads and demonstrated the proper movement.

Sarah appeared in the trading post door, drawn by Thomas's presence among the traders. But Cooper's hand on her arm kept her from interrupting.

"Let him learn," he murmured. "Standing Bear's forgotten more about survival than most of us will ever know."

Thomas tried the bow again, mimicking Standing Bear's fluid motion. The trader nodded approval, then gestured to the space beside him.

"Sit. Your sister draws pictures of us, so you should learn our ways."

Emma looked up from her journal, blushing at being caught sketching. But Standing Bear merely nodded to her. "Pictures help remember. Memory is life on the trail."

Sarah moved closer. The bundles of dried plants on one blanket caught her attention. Standing Bear's wife, Bird Who Sings, noticed her interest.

"For birthing," she said, her English forced but clear. She held up a twisted root. "Stops blood. Grows near water."

Her eyes met Sarah's. "Many places to find it if you know how to look."

Caleb emerged from Cooper's workshop, his hands dusty with repair work. Standing Bear acknowledged him with the same formal bow he'd taught Thomas.

"A man who knows wood," the trader said, touching a carved hunting bow. "This needs mending. Trade work for knowledge?"

The bow was beautiful, and its wood was bent with expert care. However, a crack had formed near one tip, threatening the weapon's integrity.

"I'd be honored," Caleb replied, examining the damage. "Though I don't know these woods like pine and oak."

"Different trees, same spirit," Standing Bear said. "Wood speaks to those who listen, no matter the forest." He selected a bundle of herbs from his blanket. "Medicine for your leg while you work. Makes old injuries remember their strength."

Sarah looked up sharply at this, but Bird Who Sings had already shown her how to prepare the herbs. "In water first," she explained. Then, wrap it with a warm cloth. It's suitable for trail walking."

Thomas had discovered Standing Bear's collection of arrow points, each a masterpiece of patient craft. The trader picked up a piece of flint and began demonstrating the basic flaking technique.

"Slow hands," he instructed. "Stone has its own heart. Must listen before you shape."

Emma's journal now contained detailed sketches of medicinal plants, each labeled with Cherokee and English names. Bird Who Sings added notes about seasonal changes and how to recognize the same plant through its different forms.

"Plants are like people," she told Emma. "Wear different clothes for different seasons. Must know them in all their shapes."

Standing Bear presented Thomas with a simple hunting knife, its handle worn smooth with use. "Tools should know their owner's hand," he said. "Practice respect first, skill follows."

Caleb worked on the bow, letting the strange wood tell him its secrets. His leg ached less with the trader's medicine.

Standing Bear strung the mended bow, testing its strength. "Good work," he said. "Wood remembers its purpose." He looked at Thomas, still practicing with his knife. "Like children remember lessons."

The sun began to fall over Independence as Cooper circled the Wheeler wagon one final time. His eye caught details Caleb might have missed – a loose bolt here, a weak seam there. Each flaw represented a potential crisis hundreds of miles from help.

"Third wheel's better," Cooper said, testing the repaired iron rim. "Should hold past Fort Laramie if you're careful. But you'll want to check these spokes every morning." He demonstrated the proper way to sound them for weakness. "Wood talks to you differently when it's tired."

Behind them, Rebecca Mills knelt in the dirt, teaching Sarah the art of trail cooking. A Dutch oven was sitting in a bed of hot coals, filling the evening air with the aroma of fresh bread.

"Fire's like a living thing out there," Rebecca explained as she stirred the hot coals. "Too hot; your bread burns while you're rationing fuel. Too cool, you're eating dough while burning double wood."

Emma sat cross-legged nearby, attempting to coax a flame from flint and steel. Her tenth attempt produced only sparks, but she remained determined.

"Smaller shavings," Cooper's son Daniel called from where he and Thomas practiced their knot tying. "Catch the spark closer to the base." Thomas's tongue poked out in concentration as he copied Daniel's movements.

"Again," Daniel said patiently. "A loose knot's worse than none – gives you false confidence."

Margaret sat in the wagon's shadow. Her doll wore a new dress fashioned from scraps Mary Mills had shared.

"Can't sleep past dawn on the trail, Miss Liberty," Margaret informed her doll with perfect mimicry of her mother's tone. "Got to be up when the stars are still out."

Emma's fire caught suddenly, tiny flames dancing among the shavings. Her triumphant smile dimmed quickly as she realized the real challenge would be keeping it alive.

"Good," Cooper said, pausing in his wagon inspection. "Now learn to do it in the wind. In the rain. In the dark when your family depends on warmth."

Thomas had graduated to splicing rope under Daniel's guidance. His first attempt was poorly frayed, but the second showed promise.

"Just like dovetails, Pa," he called to Caleb. "Got to feel how the pieces want to fit."

The comparison startled Caleb. He'd been teaching Thomas basic woodworking since the boy could hold a plane, and now those lessons were transforming into trail craft.

"Speaking of fit," Cooper said, "let's see how you've arranged your load." He climbed halfway into the wagon, testing the weight distribution. "The Medical chest needs to ride higher. Put it where you can reach it quickly."

Sarah nodded as she began rearranging.

Thomas finally mastered the splice, holding it up for Daniel's inspection. The older boy tested it with his total weight, nodding approval when it held.

"Trail's got no patience for almost good enough," he said, unconsciously echoing his father's teachings. "Every knot's got to be your best knot."

Cooper's hand fell on Caleb's shoulder. "They're learning fast," he said quietly. "That's good. The trail doesn't give much time for slow lessons."

The stars were fully out now, turning their scattered camp into a collection of firelit islands in the growing darkness. Tomorrow, they would lead morning prayers at the church one final time. Then, the true leaving would begin.

The first stars appeared as Cooper directed the Wheeler wagon into position along the forming circle. Other wagons arrived at regular intervals, each finding its place in the growing train. Lantern light reflected off the white canvas covers, making them glow in the darkness.

"Keep your back wheels aligned with the Millses'," Cooper called. Spacing is crucial. If it is too tight, you'll bog down in the weather. Too loose, you'll lose protection."

Thomas worked with Daniel Mills and other boys, establishing a network of young scouts. They ranged around the circle's edge, learning their assigned watch positions.

"Each boy's got his section," Daniel explained, showing Thomas where to stand. "You see anything – animal, Indian, storm coming – you give the signal and run to your family's wagon. No heroics."

Caleb checked their wheel alignment while Cooper explained the circle's purpose. "Storm comes up, you'll want these gaps even. Makes a windbreak. Indian trouble, you can close ranks quickly. Stampede, you've got a ready corral."

Other families continued arriving. The Blackwells' fine Conestoga wagon took its place across the circle while the modest farm wagons of the Hatfields and Clarks filled in between.

Sarah paused in her preparations, watching the community take shape. "Strange," she said softly. "Yesterday, we were strangers. Tomorrow, we trust each other with our lives."

"Trail has a way of making family from necessity," Rebecca replied. She pointed to the growing circle. "Look how the children are already forming bonds."

Indeed, age groups had naturally assembled throughout the camp. Young mothers gathered near the Mills' wagon. Older children ran errands between wagons while toddlers played.

Emma had found a quiet spot to continue her documentation, recording each wagon's position and family name. Her map showed the circle's arrangement with careful attention to detail.

"Good thinking," Cooper said, noticing her work. "Knowing your neighbors could save your life out there. Where they're from, what skills they have, which ones you can trust in crisis."

Thomas returned from his scouting lesson. "Daniel says I'm to watch the northwest section," he reported. "Says I've got good eyes for weather changes."

"Speaking of weather," Cooper pointed to the horizon. "See those clouds? Better secure everything tight tonight."

Emma made one final circuit of the circle, completing her map. Each wagon now had its place in her journal, and each family had its note about skills and needs.

"Trail's teaching already," Cooper observed, watching the camp settle into its first night together. "Tomorrow's storm will reveal who paid attention."

Soon, these families would trust their lives to each other. Tonight, they learned to be neighbors in a new way.

Caleb sat in the wagon's doorway and studied his trail notes by the light from the campfire.

Emma sat in the corner of the wagon, writing by the light of a small candle. Her letter to her grandparents tried to capture her emotions.

"Dear Grandmother and Grandfather," she wrote, her letters careful and precise. "The wagons make a circle like the pictures in my Bible storybook, where the Israelites camped in the wilderness. Thomas says he's learning to be a watchman, like in the Psalms you taught us..."

Through the canvas, they could hear Thomas practicing Standing Bear's greeting, whispering the words repeatedly. He'd arranged his new knife and rope where he could reach them quickly.

"Listen," Sarah whispered.

Beyond the wagon circle, a coyote howled in the darkness. The sound carried clear across the prairie.

Emma's letter continued steadily: "Pa studies Mr. Cooper's maps every night. Ma is learning to cook in a Dutch oven from Mrs. Mills; she says to call her Rebecca. They say titles don't matter on the trail. Thomas has a real knife now, and Margaret's doll has a new dress made from trail cloth..."

"Cooper says we'll need to be up before dawn," Caleb said as he placed a bookmark in his trail notes. "Storm coming. Wants everything secured extra tight."

Sarah finished sorting; each item was now assigned its precise place. As Cooper had advised, the medicine chest rode high, ready for quick access.

"Strange," she said, settling beside Caleb in the wagon's doorway. "Everything we are, packed up so neat and tight."

Emma carefully noted her closing lines: "Please don't worry about us. We're learning new things every day. The trail is long, but we're not alone. Other families share the circle, saying Oregon's worth the journey. Thomas says the stars will guide us truly..."

The coyote called again, closer now. In the darkness, lanterns glowed from other wagons where families held their midnight vigils. The circle stood firm against the prairie night, a temporary home for permanent wanderers.

"Time for sleep," Sarah said finally. "Dawn comes early on the trail."

Emma sealed her letter, adding it to the packet they'd leave with Cooper for the next eastbound mail. Her journal lay open beside her, recording one final observation: "First night in the circle. Thomas says we're like stars now, all of us finding our places in a new sky."

Dawn crept across the wagon circle, revealing heavy clouds building in the west. Cooper moved from wagon to wagon, checking preparations with the urgency of a man who'd seen storms swallow whole trains.

"Canvas needs another tie here," he told Caleb, testing their cover's tension. "Storm hits wrong; loose cloth can tear your whole roof off. What's left to trade for supplies?"

Caleb glanced at their remaining furniture, stacked neatly beside the wagon. Sarah's cherished writing desk, the cradle that had held all their children, his father's corner cupboard – the last pieces of their Pennsylvania life.

"Desk's good walnut," he said, touching the smooth grain. "Brass fittings still true."

Cooper nodded. "Hendricks at the trade store collects fine pieces. Might get fair value there."

"The cradle?" she asked quietly.

"Too heavy," Cooper replied, his voice gentle but firm. "Weight's death on the trail. But that cupboard's worth something – good dry goods could make the difference past South Pass."

"Wagon's riding heavy on the left," Cooper noted, rechecking their load distribution. "Might need to shift some weight. Every pound matters when you're climbing hills."

The trade store's windows gleamed as Caleb and Cooper maneuvered the desk inside. Hendricks, a thin man with merchant's careful eyes, examined each piece.

"Fine work," he admitted finally. "But heavy furniture's not moving well. Everyone's traveling light these days." His offer came low, as expected.

Sarah stood by as the cradle went next; only Emma saw her touch the carved roses one last time.

"Medical supplies," Cooper prompted, steering them toward the store's practical goods. "Extra axle wood. Dried meat's worth its weight in gold past Fort Laramie."

"Storm's coming faster than I like," Cooper said, studying the western clouds. "Need to be moving before it hits. Time for final checks."

The wagon line stretched along Independence's main street. Caleb checked their wheel one final time; the iron rim sang accurately under his knuckles, though for how many miles remained a mystery.

"Last chance to back out," Cooper said, appearing beside him with a fresh stack of maps. "Though you don't strike me as the backing out type."

Sarah secured the final knot on their cover. The canvas snapped tight against the rising wind, ready to shed the coming storm.

"Everyone in place," Cooper called, his voice carrying down the line of wagons. "Weather's pushing us out early!"

"Got everything, Thomas?" Caleb asked, watching his son reluctantly leave Standing Bear's last-minute lesson.

"Yes, sir." The boy's hand rested on his new knife, his other clutching a small packet. Standing Bear gave me some special wrapping for the blade. He says it keeps the spirit of the steel happy."

"Final checks!" Cooper's voice carried urgency now. The storm's edge was visible on the horizon, a dark line advancing across the prairie. "Once we move out, there's no running back for forgotten things!"

Sarah climbed up beside Margaret, her medicine chest secured within easy reach. Rebecca had helped her arrange everything for quick access: birth supplies near the top and fever medicines below.

"Ready?" Caleb asked quietly.

Sarah's hand found his. "Ready."

Rebecca embraced Sarah quickly, pressing a final package into her hands. "Extra yarrow," she whispered. "And Mary's doll patterns for Margaret. Some things make the trail feel shorter."

Thunder rumbled in the distance as the first wagons began to move. Wheels that had stood firm in Pennsylvania mud rolled toward unknown territories, carrying generations of hopes and fears with equal indifference.

"Stay close to the Mills," Cooper advised, walking alongside as they joined the line. "They know the trail's moods. Watch their lead in river crossings."

Margaret's voice rose above the wagon's creak: "Goodbye, street! Goodbye store! Goodbye, trading post!"

The wagon wheel rolled over Independence's boundary, the iron rim singing a different note on the prairie track. Thomas leaned out, watching their last trace of civilization disappear beneath the advancing storm.

"Look, Pa!" he called. "You can see the whole trail ahead!"

"Remember," Cooper called, his voice nearly lost in the rising wind. "Trail's got no memory for what you were. Only matters what you become!"

The storm broke as they crossed the final threshold between town and prairie. Rain fell in sheets, and the wind became more brisk.

The line of wagons moved steadily west, each revolution of the wheels carrying them further from everything known. Sarah's hand found Caleb's again as the last trace of Independence disappeared in the storm's grey curtain.

The wheel turned, the journey began, and Independence disappeared behind them, like many things they'd soon learn to live without.

5

THE GATHERING STORM

Elm Grove to Kansas River Crossing, April 1843

Caleb leaned against the wagon as he looked over Elm Grove's campground. A dozen wagons had arrived since dawn. The Blackwells were the last to arrive; their three wagons had fresh paint and brass fittings. They were pulled by matched pairs of horses that probably cost more than Caleb's entire rig.

The creak of wagon wheels drew his attention as Sarah guided their oxen into the assigned position. She held the reins with confidence, though her knuckles were white with tension. Thomas walked alongside the wagon, pointing out every prairie dog hole to Margaret, who watched from her perch atop the jockey box.

"Patched canvas won't last a week on the trail," Victoria Blackwell's voice carried from where she stood with a group of women.

Samuel Cooper stood near the center of the gathering, arranging the wagon order on a scrap of paper. The frontier guide's patched buckskins and worn rifle spoke of trail experience the Blackwells' money couldn't buy.

"Wheeler," Cooper nodded as Caleb approached. "Your wagon's set for the middle position. Strong enough to help if there's trouble ahead or behind."

"Blackwells leading?" Caleb inquired.

"Abraham insisted," Cooper replied. "Man thinks three wagons and matched horses make him trail master by right."

Before Caleb could respond, a child's scream split the morning air. He turned to see Charles Blackwell sprawled in the grass beside his family's wagon, his arm bent at an unnatural angle. Victoria's silk dress snagged on the wagon wheel as she rushed to her son.

Abraham Blackwell's voice boomed across the camp. "Someone fetch a doctor! Now!"

Sarah was already on her way, her medical chest tucked under one arm. Emma appeared with Sarah's herb bag, setting it within easy reach.

Victoria Blackwell's voice cracked with panic. "He needs a real doctor, not a midwife."

"The nearest doctor's two days back in Independence," Sarah replied, examining Charles's arm. "This is a clean break. I can set it."

Abraham Blackwell stepped forward, his city boots awkward in the prairie grass. "If anything happens to my son..."

"Then you'll want the best care available," Sarah said. "Emma, I need the willow bark tea. Charles, this will help with the pain."

Caleb watched as his wife worked. The boy's crying slowed as the willow bark took effect. Sarah gripped the boy's arm and swiftly set the bone in a single, smooth motion, drawing a gasp from Victoria Blackwell.

"Keep it still," Sarah instructed as she bound the arm with strips of clean linen. "No wagon riding for at least two days. He can rest in your cart until we reach the river."

Victoria's thanks were stiff, but her eyes exposed a new respect as she helped Charles to his feet. Abraham Blackwell said nothing but only pressed a coin into Sarah's hand before turning away. She never looked at it before placing it in her apron pocket.

Cooper called everyone together as evening came. "The Kansas River's running high," he announced. "We'll need to prepare the wagons before we attempt to cross."

"My wagons are the finest available," Abraham Blackwell quipped. "No need for crude modifications."

Caleb studied the map. "Empty barrels lashed to the wagon beds would provide flotation—better than risking the current."

"The carpenter speaks of barrels while I have the finest waterproof canvas money can buy," Blackwell scoffed. "I think we know which opinion carries more weight."

Cooper's eyes met Caleb's briefly. "We'll discuss options tomorrow after scouting the crossing. For now, it is best to secure the wagons. Storm's brewing."

The gathering dispersed as the first drops of rain began to fall. Caleb helped Sarah move her medical supplies under cover, watching as Thomas and Daniel Cooper raced between the wagons, checking horse lines and wagon covers.

Thunder rolled across the prairie as families settled in for the night. Through the wagon's canvas, Caleb heard Emma telling Margaret stories about brave pioneers, her voice steady despite the growing storm. Sarah sat quietly in the wagon, wondering what the river crossing might bring.

The rain drummed steadily on the wagon cover, but Caleb's thoughts were already on the river ahead. He'd seen how the Blackwells' fine horses spooked at thunder – they'd be worse at a water crossing. His fingers traced the smooth wood of the wagon ribs, considering how best to lash barrels for flotation, no matter what Abraham Blackwell thought of his advice.

A loud thunderclap sent Margaret scrambling into Sarah's lap. Emma's story never faltered, though her voice rose slightly to cover the storm's fury. Beneath their wagon, Thomas and Daniel Cooper had created a makeshift fort, their whispered plans for tomorrow's adventures carrying through the wagon boards.

Caleb's leg ached with the weather but pushed the discomfort aside. Tomorrow would bring its challenges. For now, his family was dry and safe, their wagon sound beneath them. The storm could rage all it wanted – they'd face the river when it came.

He caught fragments of the Blackwells' conversation through the canvas in their nearby wagon. Victoria's worried voice carried over the rain: "Abraham, perhaps we should consider the carpenter's suggestion about the barrels..."

"Nonsense," Abraham's reply was firm. "I won't have our wagons looking like some common merchant's rig. We're leading this train properly or not at all."

Sarah's hand found Caleb's in the darkness. Neither spoke, but they knew tomorrow's river crossing would test more than just wagon craftsmanship. Class pride meant little to rush water. Some lessons could only be learned the hard way.

The storm raged through the night, but it was clear and calm by dawn. Caleb rose early and checked their wagon's lashings. The ground had turned to mud, and already he could see the Blackwells' fine horses struggling with their heavy wagons.

Cooper appeared through the morning mist, his buckskins dark with dew. "River's up after that rain," he said without preamble. "Might be worth scouting a better crossing before we move the wagons."

Thomas emerged from under the wagon, his face brightening at the exploration prospect. "Can I help check for tracks, Mr. Cooper?"

"Might as well," Cooper nodded. "Your eyes are sharp enough. Daniel, you coming?"

Cooper's son grabbed his father's spare canteen, and soon, the small group disappeared into the wet grass. Caleb watched them go, noting how Thomas's stride mimicked the elder Cooper's pace.

Sarah organized her medical supplies while Emma helped Margaret dress. The girls' chatter mixed with the morning sounds of the camp—horses stamping, coffee boiling, and children calling to each other between wagons. Only the Blackwells remained apart, taking breakfast in their wagon rather than joining the communal fires.

Victoria Blackwell emerged eventually, picking her way through the mud in impractical shoes. She paused near Sarah's medical station, her manner still stiff but lacking yesterday's condescension.

"How is Charles's arm?" Sarah asked, not looking up from her work.

"The pain's manageable with your willow bark tea," Victoria admitted. "Abraham still thinks we should have waited for a proper doctor."

Sarah's hands remained steady as she packed fresh bandages. "The break will heal cleanly if he keeps it still. It's best not to let him ride in the wagon until we pass the river crossing. The jostling would only cause pain."

Victoria's fingers fiddled with the lace at her cuff. "About the crossing... Abraham's certain our wagons will manage, but after last night's rain..."

"Empty barrels are easy enough to lash on," Sarah said carefully. "Caleb could show your drivers the proper method. For the children's safety, of course."

Before Victoria could respond, a shout came from the direction of the river. Thomas and Daniel ran into camp, their boots coated in mud.

"I found a better crossing!" Thomas called out. "Mr. Cooper says the river's lower there, with a firm bottom!"

Cooper followed at a more measured pace, his experienced eyes already assessing the camp's reaction.

Abraham Blackwell emerged from his wagon, his manner making it clear he expected to be consulted first.

"The main crossing's too dangerous after the rain," Cooper announced, not waiting for Blackwell's permission to speak. "But the boys found a better ford a mile downstream. Current's slower there, and the approach is more gradual."

Blackwell's face darkened. "We've already planned our route. I won't have it changed on the word of two boys playing at being scouts."

"Might be worth checking yourself," Cooper suggested mildly. "Unless you're certain your horses can handle the main crossing in this mud."

The challenge in Cooper's voice was subtle but clear. Blackwell couldn't refuse to inspect the alternate crossing without losing face, but accepting meant acknowledging he wasn't as confident as he pretended.

"Very well," Blackwell said stiffly. "Though I expect this delay will prove unnecessary."

Emma slipped away to her hideout with Mary Mills as the men gathered for the inspection. Caleb caught fragments of their whispered conversation as he checked the wagon's wheels one final time.

"Father says the river's like life," Mary was saying. "You can't cross it proud, or it'll pull you under."

Emma's reply was thoughtful. "Ma says nature doesn't care about fancy wagons or fine horses. Only about who knows how to read her signs."

Caleb smiled slightly at his daughter's wisdom. The river ahead would test them all, but at least some children were learning the proper lessons early.

Sarah appeared at his side, her medical bag already packed for emergencies. "Victoria's worried," she said softly. "She knows Abraham's pride could cost them dearly at the crossing."

"Cooper won't let him risk the whole train," Caleb replied, though he shared her concern. "And the boys did find a better ford. I could see it in Thomas's eyes – he's learning to read the land."

Sarah's hand found his, squeezing briefly. "He's growing up out here; all of them are. Sometimes, I think that's what scares the Blackwells most. Their children learn there's more to life than money and status."

The inspection party returned before noon, Abraham Blackwell's face tight with suppressed anger. Cooper gathered the wagon masters to announce their decision, though Caleb already knew what it would be. Thomas's proud grin as he stood beside Daniel told the story enough.

"We'll take the lower crossing," Cooper announced. "Those wanting to reinforce their wagons with barrels can speak with Mr. Wheeler about proper lashing techniques. We move at first light tomorrow."

Victoria Blackwell caught Sarah's eye across the camp, her manner more uncertain than proud now. The river ahead would demand choices from all of them – about wagons and barrels, pride and practicality, and who to trust when the water rose.

The sky was cold and gray as dawn broke over the Kansas River. Caleb tested the barrel lashings on his wagon. The water churned brown and fast ahead, swollen from the recent rains.

Samuel Cooper stood at the river's edge, testing the current with a long pole. The guide's expression remained neutral, but his frequent glances at the Blackwells' lead wagon spoke volumes. Abraham Blackwell had refused the barrel reinforcements, trusting in his expensive waterproofed canvas and matched horses.

"Ready those block and tackle lines," Cooper called. "First wagon moves in ten minutes."

Thomas came to Caleb's side, his face grave as he checked the rope coils. "Daniel says the river's risen three inches since yesterday."

"That so?" Caleb reacted. "Best pay attention then. Might need those tracking skills of yours today."

Sarah finished securing their medical supplies. "Victoria's worried about Charles's arm," she said quietly. "The jostling could undo yesterday's setting."

"Blackwell's pride cost more than a broken arm if he's not careful," Caleb replied, watching the merchant's horses dance nervously at the water's edge.

The first wagon rolled forward under Cooper's direction. The Millers' rig was small and light, reinforced with Caleb's barrel system. It entered the water smoothly, the guide ropes keeping it steady against the current.

Abraham Blackwell's voice cut through the morning air. "Time to show these people how proper equipment handles the crossing. Thomas, bring our lead wagon forward."

The Blackwells' driver, a nervous man named Thomas Barnes, gripped the reins. The horses sensed his tension and tossed their heads against the bit.

"Mr. Blackwell," Cooper's voice carried a clear warning. "Best let the smaller wagons test the ford first."

"Nonsense. My wagons are twice the quality of these farm rigs. Barnes, move forward."

The lead wagon rolled toward the water, its polished wood bright against the muddy bank. Victoria Blackwell clutched Charles close as their driver urged the horses forward. The team balked at the water's edge, their hooves sliding in the mud.

"Keep them straight," Blackwell commanded, but the horses were already fighting the reins. The wagon slewed sideways, its wheels catching in the soft river bottom.

"Cut the horses loose!" Cooper shouted as the current caught the wagon's side. But Barnes froze, his hands tangled in the reins as the frightened team thrashed in the deepening water.

Caleb was moving before he could think, his leg forgotten as he splashed into the river. One wheel had dropped into a hidden hole, tipping the cargo dangerously close to the water line.

"Thomas! Daniel! Bring those guide ropes!" Cooper's voice cracked like a whip. The boys responded instantly, dragging heavy coils through the shallows.

Victoria's scream pierced the air as Charles tumbled against the wagon's side, his splinted arm taking the impact. The wagon lurched deeper, water seeping through the canvas.

"Told you we needed barrels," Caleb muttered, reaching the listing wagon. "Cooper! We need to stabilize this side before we unhitch!"

The guide was already there, his buckskins dark with river water. "Boys, secure those lines to the high side. Mr. Blackwell, get your family out! Now!"

For once, Abraham Blackwell offered no argument. He helped Victoria and Charles crawl carefully toward the rear gate.

The next few minutes passed in a blur of cold water and straining ropes. Caleb writhed in pain as he helped position the logs they used as levers, but he gritted his teeth and kept working. The wagon's contents might still be saved if they could keep it from tipping further.

"Steady now," Cooper called. "Thomas, Daniel – take up that slack slowly. Wheeler, ready with the block and tackle."

The guide rope drew tight, helping stabilize the wagon's dry side while Caleb and Cooper attached the heavy pulleys.

"All together now," Cooper commanded. "Heave!"

Slowly, agonizingly, the Blackwells' lead wagon lifted from its deadly lean.

Barnes finally managed to free the frightened horses, leading them back to shore with shaking hands. Despite the cold water, the animals were lathered with sweat, and the river had ruined their harnesses.

Victoria clutched Charles on the bank, her silk dress plastered to her shoulders. The boy's splint had held, but he was in severe pain. Sarah was already beside them, checking on his injury.

Abraham Blackwell stood silent, watching his prize wagon drain river water through its expensive canvas. The carefully packed cargo must be dried, and the wood must be treated to prevent warping. His other two wagons waited on the bank, their drivers nervous about attempting the crossing.

"Mr. Wheeler," Blackwell's voice cracked slightly. "About those barrel reinforcements..."

Caleb nodded, not trusting himself to speak through chattering teeth. His leg felt like iron in the cold river, but they had five more wagons to cross before dark. Pride could wait – survival came first.

Each wagon crossed slowly, guided by the ropes held by other men in the train. By that afternoon, the final wagon was safely across.

Cooper gathered them for a brief rest. "Nature's given us her first real test," he said. "Won't be the last."

"Father says we should have listened about the barrels," Charles said quietly. "Maybe there's more to learn out here than we thought."

Victoria Blackwell approached their wagon. "Mrs. Wheeler... Sarah. Might I learn more about those willow bark preparations? For Charles's comfort, of course."

"Of course," Sarah replied, making space on the wagon step. "Emma, bring my herb box, please."

As Caleb checked their wagon's wheels, he noticed where the river crossing had stressed the wood. They'd need to make repairs before moving on.

A distant rumble of thunder echoed in the distance. Cooper's shout was immediate. "Everyone get to your wagons and secure those lines!"

The first rain fell as everyone rushed to protect their belongings. Sarah and Victoria helped Charles back to the Blackwell's wagon.

"Thomas! Daniel!" Cooper's voice carried above the growing storm. "Check those horse lines! The weather's spooking them!"

Rain drummed against the wagon canvas as Caleb secured their final ties. As he turned to help Cooper, his leg nearly buckled, but Sarah's hand caught his arm.

"Inside," she ordered. "You've done enough today."

Thunder cracked overhead as Caleb grudgingly climbed into their wagon. Emma had already arranged their bedding. Thomas and Daniel could be heard finalizing the horse lines before diving into their wagons.

"Just like the river," Margaret whispered as another thunderclap shook the wagon. "All wild and loud."

"But we're safe and dry," Emma assured her. "The river didn't beat us, nor will this storm."

A horse screamed in terror as lightning split the sky. Caleb heard Cooper shouting directions to the boys through the rain as they fought to calm the panicked animals.

"Samuel Cooper says a storm like this means we're truly on the trail now," Emma said softly, "Says it's nature's way of teaching us respect."

Sarah added to the thought. "Seems we're learning all sorts of lessons today."

A crack of splintering wood carried through the storm. Victoria Blackwell's voice rose in alarm from their wagon. "Abraham! The chest!"

Caleb grabbed his coat, but Sarah's hand stopped him. "Your leg won't hold in this mud. Let others handle it."

Before she finished speaking, they heard Thomas and Daniel splashing through the darkness, responding to the Blackwells' call. Cooper's voice guided the boys as they worked to secure whatever had broken loose.

The wagon shook with another thunderclap. Margaret burrowed into Sarah's lap. Caleb caught activity fragments through the canvas as families fought to protect their belongings from wind and rain.

"Wheeler!" Abraham Blackwell's voice barely carried through the storm. "We need you over here!"

Sarah's grip tightened on Caleb's arm, but he was already moving. "Won't be but a minute," he promised, ducking into the rain.

Lightning revealed the scene at the Blackwells' wagon. Their damaged chest had broken free of its lashings, nearly punching through the weakened canvas. Thomas and Daniel braced it with their shoulders while Cooper directed Abraham to secure new ropes.

Caleb surveyed the damage quickly, and his carpenter's knowledge provided solutions. "Need to redistribute the weight. That corner's too heavy for wet wood."

They worked together in the storm, lightning their only illumination. Abraham Blackwell's fine coat offered no protection against the rain, but he followed Caleb's instructions without complaint. The boys held steady despite the wind's buffeting.

"Secure enough for now," Caleb said finally, checking the last rope. "But that chest needs better bracing come morning."

"I'll see to it," Abraham replied, his voice carrying an unfamiliar note of respect. "Cooper says you know wagon craft better than most."

Lightning flashed again as Caleb made his way back to their wagon. His leg nearly died in the mud, but Thomas appeared beside him, offering silent support.

Sarah had hot tea waiting as Caleb climbed inside. Emma wrung out his coat while Margaret pressed close, sharing warmth. The storm raged on, but their wagon held steady, protected by experience earned through rivers and pride swallowed when needed.

"The Blackwells' horses are calmer now," Thomas reported.

The night passed with intermittent thunder and lightning throughout. Each family stayed huddled in their wagons. Class distinctions meant little now.

6

FEVER DREAMS

Kansas Territory, Late May 1843

The sun beat against Caleb's back as he watched Emma stumble on her third trip to the creek. The water bucket tipped, spilling across the dusty ground. She straightened, took two steps, and collapsed.

"Emma!" Sarah dropped her washing and rushed forward. She pressed her hand to Emma's forehead, then jerked it back. "She's burning up."

Caleb raced to their side. Emma's skin was hot to his touch, and her eyes unfocused. He lifted her, feeling the heat through her dress, and carried her toward their wagon.

Sarah cleared the wagon bed, spreading a clean blanket to lay her on. She moved quickly to check Emma's pulse, but Caleb could see the tremor in her fingers.

"The symptoms?" He kept his voice steady.

"Like Mother's journal described." Sarah pulled her medical chest from beneath the wagon seat. "Trail fever. We need to break her temperature before—" She stopped, unpacking her notes and trying to remain calm.

Rebecca Mills appeared at the wagon gate. "Sarah, let me help prepare the wagon. James can move our supplies to make room."

Thomas hovered at the edge of the group, his usual restlessness replaced with worry. "Pa? The main train's starting to move."

Caleb turned. The wagon train was already pulling away from their position. Cooper rode back through the line to assess their situation.

"How long?" Cooper asked, though his tone said he already knew.

"Five days, if we're lucky." Sarah didn't look up from Emma's flushed face. "A week if the fever holds."

Cooper nodded. "I'll mark the trail clear. James Davis knows this territory - he'll help you navigate once she's stable." He pulled a roll of red cloth from his saddlebag. "Thomas, take these marker flags. You remember how to set them?"

Thomas grabbed the flags. "Yes, sir. High and visible, tied proper so they'll hold in the wind."

"Good lad." Cooper's eyes met Caleb's. "The main train can't wait, but you'll have signs to follow."

The other wagons rumbled past, creating distance with each turn of their wheels. Margaret pressed against Caleb's leg as she watched the train disappear.

Rebecca Mills organized the remaining families. "James Davis, your family has the best hunters. Work with Peter on food rotation. Martha Peterson, help me with water purification - we'll need extra with the sick wagon."

The five wagons formed a protective circle as the main train vanished beyond the horizon. Sarah converted their wagon into a sick bay, hanging canvas for shade.

"Trail fever took my sister in '32," Martha Peterson said as she helped Sarah prepare willow bark tea. "But she didn't have a proper healer with her."

Caleb secured the wagon circle's perimeter. Thomas and Peter Davis followed behind the main train as it departed and set marker flags at half-mile intervals, learning the land's patterns.

The night fell heavy and hot. Emma's breathing turned ragged as Sarah applied cool cloths to her skin. Margaret curled in the corner of the sick wagon, whispering stories to Miss Liberty while her sister fought the fever.

"Like baby James?" Margaret's small voice carried in the darkness.

Caleb and Sarah both paused what they were doing.

"No, sweetness," Sarah replied. "Emma's stronger than the fever. She needs time to fight it."

Dawn brought no relief from the heat. Thomas returned from his morning flag check. "The main train's dust is still visible," he reported. "Heading due west."

Rebecca Mills organized the women into working shifts to share the burden of caring for Emma.

James Davis returned from hunting with a brace of rabbits hanging from his belt. "The trail's marked clear for ten miles ahead. The grass is good and the water's reliable. We can hold here while needed."

Caleb nodded. Five wagons could survive here if they worked together. Suppose Emma's fever broke in time if the water held out. If the hunting remained good.

The day passed in a haze of heat and worry. Thomas threw himself into his new responsibilities, working with Peter Davis to maintain their marking system. The boys returned covered in dust but proud of their contribution.

"Pa?" Thomas asked as they checked the horses for the night. "Will the main train wait for us?"

"They'll leave signs," Caleb replied, testing a lead rope. "Cooper knows his business."

Margaret spent the day helping Rebecca Mills with the Morton baby, though her eyes constantly strayed to the sick wagon where Emma lay.

The second night brought no relief. Emma thrashed against Sarah's attention, her skin hot enough to warm the wagon boards beneath her. "Sarah." Caleb touched her shoulder. "Rest. Martha can watch for an hour."

"I can't." Sarah's voice cracked. "If I miss the signs... if I make a mistake with the dosage..."

"Like with James?" The words slipped out before he could stop them.

Sarah paused and answered, "That was different. We didn't have Mothers' journals then, so we didn't know what to watch for."

But they both heard the fear behind her words. Trail fever could take even the most robust child, just as winter fever had taken their son. All their medical knowledge meant nothing if the body couldn't fight.

A soft thump made them turn. Margaret stood in the wagon entrance, her doll dangling from one hand.

"Emma needs her," Margaret said with a child's certainty. "Miss Liberty remembers how to fight fevers."

Sarah gathered their youngest close, pressing a kiss to her tangled curls. "Of course she does, sweet one. Just like she helps you be brave."

Caleb lifted Margaret into the wagon, watching as she tucked her precious doll beside Emma's hot fingers.

The long night was marked by Emma's labored breathing and Sarah's quiet prayers. Outside, the wagon circle stood guard against the darkness.

Thomas slept beneath the wagon. In the morning, he'd set out again with Peter, keeping himself busy while waiting for his sister to heal.

The third day dawned hotter than the last. Caleb checked the dropping levels of the water barrels.

James Davis stood nearby with his rifle ready. "The game is moving north," he reported. "Following the cooler air. We'll need to venture further today."

Sarah's voice cried from the sick wagon. "The fever's spiking. Rebecca, I need more willow bark."

Caleb ran to her side as fast as he could. Emma was thrashing about as she fought the fever, her skin hot and flushed.

"Mother wrote about cases like this," Sarah said. "When standard remedies fail, there's a more robust preparation.

Martha Peterson came with fresh water. "My sister's fever broke with whiskey compresses. Some thought it wasteful, but she lived."

Rebecca Mills took charge of Margaret, leading her away from Emma's fevered cries. "Come help with baby Morton. He needs his blanket washed."

Caleb worked steadily through the morning. His hands completed each task while his mind circled endlessly around the sick wagon. Every sound from Emma pulled at him, but he forced himself to continue working. The miniature train's survival depended on maintaining a routine.

Near noon, Thomas and Peter returned from their marking expedition. Thomas clutched something in his hand, and his face was pale.

"Found this by the creek," he said, holding a small wooden cross. "Fresh dirt. Someone else's wagon..."

Caleb took the crude marker, reading the roughly carved dates—another family's loss.

"That's why we stayed behind, Pa? So Emma won't need..."

"Go help Mr. Davis with the hunting snares," Caleb said. He tucked the cross into his pocket, away from young eyes.

The afternoon heat grew unbearable. Sarah tried every remedy she knew of, becoming increasingly desperate as Emma's fever refused to break. Rebecca Mills organized the women into prayer shifts, their whispered words mixing with Emma's restless murmurs.

Martha Peterson took the evening watch, allowing Sarah a few hours' rest. The older woman's gnarled fingers changed cool cloths and carefully measured medicine.

"Fever's a battlefield," she told Caleb as he checked on Emma. "Takes its own time to win or lose. All we can do is give her strength for the fight."

The night fell heavy across the wagon circle. Thomas slept beneath the Davis wagon, closer to Peter than their own. The boys had formed a tight bond during their time together.

A commotion broke the pre-dawn quiet. Sarah cried out with fear. "Emma! Hold her still!"

Caleb reached the wagon as Emma convulsed, her skin burning impossibly hot. Sarah worked fiercely, forcing willow bark tea between Emma's clenched teeth.

"The strongest remedy," Sarah said, her voice cracking. "Mother's last resort."

Rebecca Mills pressed a cold cloth to Emma's forehead. "We're with you, Sarah. Whatever you need."

Margaret appeared at the wagon gate, "Angels took baby James," she whispered. "They can't take Emma, too."

Caleb swept Margaret away before she saw Emma twist against another convulsion. Sarah's hands shook as she measured the final remedy.

At mid-morning, the main train's captain rode up and pulled his horse to a stop. "Cooper sent me back. The train's making good time. We can't afford to slow down with winter coming."

Caleb looked up from the water barrel he was filling. "Emma's fever hasn't broken."

"The trail's dangerous for small groups," the captain replied. "Indians, bandits, weather. Five wagons won't have much protection."

"There's no Oregon worth more than my daughter's life."

The captain shifted in his saddle. "You have three days. Any longer, the distance will be too great to make up before winter."

The small council gathered as the captain rode away. James Davis cleaned his rifle while speaking. "My family's staying. Peter's learning too much from Thomas to leave now."

Rebecca Mills nodded. "The Mortons need Sarah's help with the baby. We'll stay."

Martha Peterson's aged voice carried quiet authority. "I've survived worse than trail delays. We leave no one behind."

The five families formalized their pact as the sun rose. Once Emma recovered, they would travel together, watching each other's children and sharing their resources.

Sarah worked through the day as exhaustion took its toll. The last of her mother's remedies went into Emma's medicine in desperate hope.

The evening brought a cold wind, the first break in the heat wave. Sarah collapsed beside Emma's blankets, her strength finally giving out. Rebecca Mills and Martha Peterson took over watch duties, keeping a close eye on both.

Caleb caught Thomas studying his trail maps by lamplight. "Show me what you've learned," he said, sitting beside his son.

Thomas pointed out landmarks. "Peter and I found a better water source to the north. Marked it clear with flags."

"You're learning the land well."

"Had to, Pa." Thomas's voice carried new maturity. "Emma needs us to know the way home."

The night passed slowly. Margaret curled against Sarah's side while they slept. The Morton baby finally quieted, his mother's worried vigil matching theirs.

Dawn broke gray and cool. The first drops of rain hit the wagon canvas as Emma's fever finally broke. Sarah's hands shook as she felt her daughter's cooler skin, tears mixing with the rain that penetrated the wagon's seams.

Rain drummed against the wagon canvas as Emma opened her eyes. The fever had left her weak, but her gaze was clear for the first time in days. Sarah pressed a cup of broth to her lips, every movement gentle.

"Thomas?" Emma's voice cracked. "He's supposed to help with the morning water..."

"Rest," Sarah whispered. "Thomas has Peter to help him now."

Caleb stepped away from the wagon. He looked up to the sky and closed his eyes, letting the cold rain wash the fear from his face. James Davis approached, rifle slung across his back.

"Need to plan our route," Davis said. "Main train's four days ahead now."

They spread the map beneath the wagon awning. Thomas and Peter joined them, and their knowledge of local water sources proved invaluable. During Emma's fever, the boys had grown in responsibility, and practical skills replaced their childhood games.

Rebecca Mills organized the women into travel preparations while Martha Peterson mixed strengthening tonics for Emma. The Morton baby fussed in his mother's arms, his cries stronger after a night of rest.

"We'll follow the creek north," Thomas said, pointing to his marker flags on the map. "Better water, more game. Can meet the main train's path after the ridge."

Caleb studied his son's plan. "Cooper taught you well."

"Peter helped," Thomas replied. "He's good at reading water signs."

The rain continued through the morning, turning the prairie grass green again. Emma slept more naturally now, her breathing steady. Sarah finally allowed herself proper rest, curled beside her daughter.

James Davis and Caleb worked out the details of their new route. Once they started, five wagons could move faster than the main train, assuming they avoided trouble. The boys' marker flags would guide them.

"Emma's awake again," Rebecca called softly. "Asking for her journal."

Caleb found the leather-bound book beneath Emma's travel chest. Water stains marked several pages, but her careful handwriting remained clear. She'd documented everything until the fever took her - weather patterns, creek depths, trail signs.

"Here." He placed the journal in Emma's weak hands. "You've got some catching up to do."

Emma's fingers traced the last entry. "How far behind are we?"

"Don't worry about that now."

"I heard the captain, Pa. Four days is a long time to make up."

Caleb squeezed her hand. "We've got good people with us. Strong hunters, smart trackers. We'll find our way."

The rain eased by afternoon. Thomas and Peter made one final marking run, checking their flags against the coming journey. They returned with news of fresh game trails and clear water.

Sarah reviewed their medical supplies, noting what they'd used during Emma's fever. The women worked together seamlessly now; five families had become one through the crisis.

"The Morton baby's stronger," Margaret reported, helping Rebecca Mills fold clean blankets. "Miss Liberty says he just needed time, like Emma."

Caleb watched his youngest daughter work. She moved between wagons with quiet purpose, delivering water and messages and offering Miss Liberty's comfort to any child who needed it. The fever crisis had changed her, too, adding maturity well beyond her years.

The evening brought clearing skies and the first strategy council of their new train. James Davis laid out hunting schedules while Rebecca Mills planned supply distribution.

"Cooper marked the trail clear," Thomas said. "Peter and I can follow his signs and find the best water."

Sarah sat beside Emma, resting a hand on her daughter's forehead.

"I can write while we move," Emma whispered.

"You'll rest now," Sarah replied. "There will be time to write once you're stronger."

The night settled quietly. Margaret curled beside Emma, sharing her warmth while Sarah mixed the last of the strengthening tonics. Thomas spread his blanket beneath the Davis wagon again, but Caleb understood.

Caleb made one final check of their wagon's wheels. Emma's fever had delayed them, but every family had chosen to stay, to risk winter's approach rather than leave someone behind. They'd make up the lost time somehow, following the markers until they rejoined the main train.

Emma's voice carried soft from the wagon as she drifted toward sleep. "Will we catch them, Pa?"

"We'll make our way," Caleb replied. "Rest now. Tomorrow's soon enough to start."

7

THUNDER ON THE PLAINS

Nebraska Territory to Fort Laramie, June 1843

Thomas awoke in the early hours of the morning to a shocking new noise.

He crept onto the jockey box and saw a black dust cloud overhead. It got stronger and stronger in the seconds that passed.

"Pa!" Thomas cried and dropped. "Pa, something's coming!"

Caleb was already awake and tinkering with the wagon's wheels and axles. He stood up at Thomas' call.

The dust clouds grew more prominent, and now they could hear it clearly - a deep rumble like continuous thunder. James Davis appeared from the morning shadows, his rifle ready.

"Buffalo," Davis said quietly. "Whole herd moving north. Thomas, wake everyone in the wagon circle. Now."

Thomas ran between the five wagons and alerted everyone as quickly as possible. "Mr. Davis says circle up! Buffalo is coming!"

Sarah came out of their wagon with Margaret in her arms. "Emma, help secure the wagon!"

The thunder grew louder. Caleb helped Davis position the wagons into a defensive formation. One of the wheels on Morton's wagon caught on a rock and cracked with a barely audible sound in the chaos.

"The wheel's gone!" John Morton yelled. "Wheeler, we need-"

"No time!" Davis cut him off. "Everyone under the wagons! They're coming!"

Emma worked quickly, binding the medical chest tight against their wagon frame. Her fingers flew through the knots Thomas had taught her, checking each one twice.

The ground shook as the first buffalo appeared through the dust—massive, dark shapes moving fast. Their passage bent the prairie grass flat. The wagons creaked as the herd split around its circle, a living river of muscle and bone.

Sarah pressed Margaret's face against her shoulder, whispering prayers into her daughter's hair. Emma huddled beside them; her body curved protectively around the medical supplies.

The Morton wagon listed dangerously on its broken wheel. John Morton's face held a fearful expression as he braced against the wagon bed. His wife clutched their baby, her eyes squeezed shut.

Minutes seemed like hours until the herd passed. The thunder faded slowly, and the dust settled.

"Check for injuries," Sarah called, already moving toward the Morton wagon. "Emma, bring my supplies."

Caleb examined the broken wheel. The spokes had shattered completely, and the rim was bent. John Morton stood nearby, visibly angry.

"We had that wheel checked at Fort Kearney," he said. "Paid good money for it, too."

"Fort Kearney work's not worth spit," Davis replied. "Need a proper wheelwright, or-"

"Or a carpenter?" Morton's voice held an edge. "Like the one who helped us circle up so fast the wheel caught?"

Caleb turned away from the charge, focusing on the broken spokes. They'd need a complete replacement, and their spare wheel had been traded two weeks before for medical equipment.

Thomas stood at his elbow, excitement radiating across his face. "Did you see them, Pa? I counted-"

"Thomas." Caleb's voice stopped him. "Check our wheels—all of them. Davis, we've got to get moving before scavengers catch up with the herd.

"The wheel's beyond fixing," Caleb announced finally. "We'll need to trade at Fort Laramie."

"Three days of hard travel," Davis said. "If we move now."

John Morton's face darkened. "Three days? With a broken wheel?"

"We'll redistribute the weight," Caleb replied. "Spread your cargo among our wagons. The axle should hold if we're careful."

"Should?" Morton stepped closer. "My family's lives depend on should?"

Sarah's voice cut through the tension. "John, Mary needs water. The buffalo crossing stirred up the creek. Thomas, would you and Peter check upstream for a clear spot?"

Thomas grabbed his tracking kit and whistled for Peter Davis.

"Take watch positions," Davis called as the boys disappeared into the grass. "Buffalo mess brings wolves. Catherine, Samuel - help the Mortons shift their load."

The sun climbed higher, burning off the last dust from the buffalo passage. Thomas and Peter returned with water and news of clear trails north. Thomas clutched something in his hand - fresh tracking signs he was learning to read.

"Pawnee markers," he explained. "They're following the herd north."

Davis examined the signs. "Good eye. We'll want to parallel their trail - they know the best water this time of year."

The wagon train moved out slowly, the Morton wagon limping on its broken wheel. Thomas and Peter rode ahead on Davis's spare horses. Caleb watched them until they disappeared into the tall prairie grass.

Emma rode beside him on the jockey box, her journal open despite the jolting path. "Pa? Will the buffalo come back?"

"Not likely. They're moving north for summer grazing."

She made another note, her handwriting steady despite the wagon's movement. "The Mortons are afraid."

"Fear makes people say things they don't mean."

"Like when Thomas got chicken pox, and Ma said she'd sell him to the gypsies?"

Caleb smiled despite himself. "Something like that."

The afternoon heat built slowly. Sarah dozed in the wagon bed and Margaret curled against her side. The Morton wagon creaked behind them, but the redistributed weight kept the axle stable.

Thunder rolled in the distance—real thunder this time, not buffalo hooves. Davis called a halt to secure the wagons before the storm hit. They'd learned to read the weather since leaving Independence, and each family knew their tasks without discussion.

Thomas and Peter hadn't returned. Caleb scanned the horizon, measuring the storm's approach against the boys' absence. Davis noticed his concern.

"They know to shelter if the weather turns," Davis said. "Peter's got good sense."

But as the first drops fell, Peter Davis rode into camp alone.

"Thomas went to check a creek crossing," Peter gasped, rain plastering his hair to his forehead. "Said he saw signs of fresh water. I told him to wait, but-"

"How long ago?" Davis demanded.

"Hour, maybe? The storm came up so fast..."

Caleb was already moving, but Davis caught his arm. "Not alone. Catherine, Samuel - help the women secure the wagons. Martha, Rebecca - keep the little ones close. John, you're with us."

Even Morton's anger faded against the crisis. He grabbed his rifle and fell beside Davis as they rode into the storm.

Thunder cracked overhead as they rode into the gathering dark. Thomas had good training, Davis's lessons, and his father's stubbornness. He'd survive. He had to.

The prairie stretched endless in the storm, the grass bending under the wind. Caleb forced himself to read the signs—broken stalks showing recent passage, muddy prints telling direction.

Peter's voice carried between thunderclaps. "There! By the creek crossing!"

They found Thomas' tracking kit half-buried in mud. Thomas, however, was gone.

The storm lasted through the night. As the sun rose, Davis separated the men into search parties. Two men were assigned to go south, two more north, and the rest to guard the wagons.

Caleb didn't find the tracks indicating where Thomas had seen others until mid-morning. They were moving north.

His heart sank, remembering the warnings about Indian contact. But the tracks showed no signs of struggle, and Thomas had been learning Pawnee words from the trading posts.

A horse whinnied behind him. Caleb turned to find a mounted warrior watching from the grass - young, but his face painted for hunting. The warrior raised his hand in greeting, speaking careful English.

"The boy who reads signs," he said. "He is safe."

Relief hit Caleb like a physical blow. "Where?"

"With Swift Fox. Learning buffalo medicine." The warrior pointed north. "We bring him when the sun touches that hill."

True to their word, the Pawnee hunters appeared at sunset. Thomas rode double with a warrior he called Swift Fox, his face smudged with dust but his eyes bright with adventure. He rattled off Pawnee words as Sarah checked him for injuries, explaining how Swift Fox had found him studying buffalo sign.

"He says I read tracks like Pawnee children," Thomas reported proudly. "Said the stars guided me to them."

One of the hunters had taken an arrow wound from a rival tribe. Sarah traded medical care for buffalo meat, her gentle hands bridging the language barrier. Thomas translated what he could, his small store of Pawnee words growing with each exchange.

The morning's tensions were forgotten, and the five families shared a feast of fresh buffalo meat. Even John Morton's anger faded as he learned the Pawnee knew a faster route to Fort Laramie. Thomas sat with the hunters, soaking up their words like prairie soil taking rain.

They were three days from Fort Laramie, and the Morton wagon was barely holding together. Thomas finally slept, and Swift Fox's teachings restored and expanded his tracking kit. Tomorrow would bring new challenges, but tonight, they rested, knowing that some treasures couldn't be measured in Fort Laramie gold.

Dawn would decide what to trade and keep and which treasures to sacrifice for survival. But tonight, they slept in the circle of wagons, surrounded by the night sounds of the prairie. Whatever Fort Laramie demanded, they would face it together.

Fort Laramie's walls rose yellow against the morning sky. Caleb stood with James Davis and John Morton, studying the fort's activity through trail dust. Supply wagons crowded the entrance, their drivers haggling with stone-faced traders.

"Prices are worse than we expected," Davis said quietly. "Four dollars for flour that cost one in Independence."

Morton shifted uneasily. "Maybe the Pawnee trade route-"

"Tribe's moved north with the buffalo." Davis checked his rifle's load. "Fort's our only choice for that wheel."

"The Kendricks traded their mirror for half-weight in flour," Emma reported. "And Mrs. Peterson says they're not taking bank notes anymore. Only gold or trade goods."

Caleb studied his daughter's figures. She'd organized their remaining trade goods by likely value - tools they could spare, Sarah's preserved fruit, even Thomas's old winter coat. But the total fell far short of Fort Laramie's prices.

The Morton wagon creaked ominously behind them. Three days of careful travel had worn the makeshift repairs thin. The broken wheel barely held together, forcing them to move at half speed while storms threatened.

"We'll try the trade office first," Davis decided. Morton, bring your wife's jam—it might sweeten them up some."

Thomas rode up on Davis's spare horse, his face dark with trail dust. "Soldiers at the north gate are trading better," he reported. "And there's a wheelwright inside who needs medicine for his boy."

Sarah looked up from sorting her medical supplies. Her chest felt lighter now—there had been too many fevers and accidents since Independence. She'd been rationing herbs, saving the most vital medicines for desperate needs.

"What's wrong with the boy?"

"Saw him coughing. Like Cooper's son last summer, before you helped."

Sarah's fingers found the small packet of fever bark - her last portion, saved for Margaret if the summer heat brought sickness.

"Shaw's trading post first," Davis said. "He knows Cooper - might honor old debts."

They left the women organizing camp, with Thomas and Peter standing guard with borrowed rifles. The fort's interior hummed with activity—traders arguing in three languages, soldiers playing cards in doorways, and the sound of money changing hands everywhere.

Shaw's trading post squatted near the fort's center, its shelves stacked with essential goods. The trader stood behind a broad counter, wearing Independence clothes that were gone yellow with prairie dust.

"Wheel's forty dollars gold," Shaw announced after examining their broken rim. "Thirty with the carpenter's plane in trade."

Caleb's fingers tightened on his grandfather's plane - the last Wheeler tools, five generations of craft worn smooth in its handle. Morton's face went slack at the price.

"Highway robbery," Davis growled.

"Highway's free," Shaw replied quickly. "My fort, my prices."

They tried three more traders, each quoting higher prices. The wheelwright needed medicine but wouldn't bargain down. By noon, the fort's sun had burned away all options but the hardest.

Emma waited at the gate, her face showing she'd already read their failure. "I made new lists," she said, stepping beside Caleb. "If we share the Davis wagon's space and redistribute the Morton's load again..."

"Won't work uphill," Davis cut in. "Not with storms coming."

Emma's chin lifted. "Then we trade smart. The Kendricks told me-"

"Emma." Caleb stopped her gently. "This needs fixing properly, not patching."

"Like Ma says about setting bones?" Her voice went quiet. "Sometimes proper hurts worse?"

Sarah met them at the camp's edge. One look at their faces told her everything. Without comment, she went to her medicine chest and removed the fever bark packet.

"Sarah-" Caleb started.

"We need that wheel," she said. "The bark regenerates. Skills matter more than supplies."

Emma was already debating the possibilities. "If we trade Ma's medicine and Pa's plane, plus the preserved fruit and Thomas's coat..."

"And this." Caleb pulled their family Bible from the wagon. The leather binding was worn smooth by generations of hands, and its pages were marked with Wheeler's births and deaths. Sarah's fingers whitened on the medicine packet.

"Not the Bible," she whispered. "Caleb, it's all we have left of-"

"Got no choice." His voice came rougher than intended. "Can't risk the Morton wagon failing in mountain territory."

"I'll help trade," she said. "I've been learning values, and Mr. Davis says girls can bargain harder because men don't expect it."

Caleb started to refuse, but Sarah's hand on his arm stopped him. Their daughter had matured immensely since Independence. Maybe it was time to trust that growth.

Shaw's face showed surprise when Emma stepped up to his counter. She carefully laid out their goods: medical supplies, a carpenter's plane, preserved fruit, a winter coat, and the family Bible.

"For the wheel," she said clearly. "Plus three cups of flour and a bottle of laudanum for my mother's medical chest."

Shaw laughed. "Girl, that wheel's worth-"

"Worth forty dollars gold." Emma opened her journal. "But you traded Pete Wilson a wheel for thirty in mixed value last week. And the fever bark is worth fifteen to any fort doctor, especially with summer coming."

She pointed to Sarah's careful label on the medicine packet. "From Catherine Barrett's supply. Every fort doctor knows that name."

Shaw's eyes narrowed. "Catherine Barrett's dead."

"Her daughter isn't." Emma's voice stayed steady. "And she's trading you better than fort prices because we're fair people with honest goods."

The bargaining took another hour. Emma never raised her voice or lost her figures, measuring each trade against her careful lists. Ultimately, they got the wheel for the plane, medicine, preserved fruit, and half the Bible's asking price.

"Keep it," Shaw said gruffly, pushing the Bible across his counter. "Bad luck to trade Scripture anyway."

They left Fort Laramie as sunset painted its walls red. The new wheel ran true beneath the Morton wagon, and Sarah's medical chest carried fresh laudanum.

Emma rode beside Caleb on the jockey box. She'd organized the children into hunting parties like Thomas's

Pawnee friends, teaching them to read buffalo signs. Even Margaret helped now, sorting prairie flowers for Sarah's medical stores.

"Shaw wasn't so hard," Emma said finally. "Once I showed him my figures."

Caleb touched the Bible in his pocket. "You did good work today."

"Had to, Pa. The trail takes what it needs. We have to make sure it doesn't take what matters most."

Behind them, Thomas was teaching Peter more Pawnee words. Sarah treated the Morton boy's cough with her new laudanum. The wagon train moved steadily west, five families stronger for knowing what they'd trade and what they'd protect.

8

THE SILENT SUMMER

South Pass Region, July 1843

The morning sun crept over South Pass as Caleb looked over the wagon. His fingers found wear in the iron rims—not critical yet, but concerning after Fort Laramie's prices. The mountain air was a bit cold despite July's promise of heat.

Rebecca Mills's cough shattered the dawn quiet. The sound struck wrong—too wet, too deep. Caleb turned to see her stumble against her wagon wheel, a water bucket dropping from her limp fingers.

"Sarah!" The name tore from his throat before he could stop it.

Sarah appeared from their wagon to Rebecca's side. Her quick steps faltered as she reached her. One touch to the woman's forehead and Sarah's face went still as it had during the fever epidemic.

"Get her inside," Sarah commanded. "Emma, bring my mother's journal. Thomas! Warn the other wagons. No one comes close until I say."

Caleb lifted Rebecca as gently as he could. The woman's skin burned against his hands, and her breath rattled wet in her chest. James Mills appeared from their wagon, sleep still clouding his eyes.

"What's wrong with Ma?" Mary Mills pushed past her father, reaching for Rebecca's hand.

"Back, Mary." Sarah's voice carried the sharp edge of fear. "Everyone back. Emma, here are the isolation procedures from Grandmother's notes. Now."

Emma moved frighteningly efficiently for a ten-year-old, marking boundaries with rope and setting wash basins where Sarah directed. She'd learned too much about sickness since Independence.

Thomas ran between wagons, shouting warnings. His voice cracked with urgency: "No one comes close! Ma says stay back!"

Sarah worked without rest, checking symptoms against her notes. The journal's pages had grown thin with use.

"Cholera," Sarah said finally, her voice tight. "Like Mother described from the ship crossings. We need to isolate everyone who's had contact."

James Mills paced outside the boundary ropes, his rifle forgotten against the wagon wheel. "What can I do?"

"Pray," Sarah replied, though her hands never stopped moving. "And keep Mary away. Children catch it quickest."

The sun climbed higher, burning away the mountain chill. Caleb supervised the isolation shelters, ensuring every family had clean water and separate facilities. His leg ached from the constant movement, but he pushed through it.

Margaret hadn't spoken since Rebecca's collapse. She sat in the wagon door, watching Mary Mills beg Emma for news about her mother.

Mary Mills fell ill as sunset painted the mountains red. Her tiny body burned with fever as James Mills watched helplessly from beyond the quarantine line. Rebecca's cough grew worse, each breath a battle against fluid-filled lungs.

The night brought no relief. Sarah stayed at Rebecca's bedside while Emma tended other patients. Thomas searched the mountainside for herbs Sarah needed.

Thunder rolled across South Pass as midnight neared. Rebecca Mills died as the first drops fell, her hand clasped in Sarah's grip. The storm swallowed her final words – something about Mary's quilt, still unfinished in their wagon.

Sarah's composure cracked as Emma helped wash Rebecca's body. Mother and daughter clung together in the sick wagon, their grief muffled by thunder and rain.

Outside, Thomas dug graves with James Mills, the boy's small shoulders straight against the storm.

The memorial service was brief. Caleb's voice cracked as he read from their family Bible - the one Shaw hadn't taken at Fort Laramie. Margaret stood silent beside Emma.

They continued their push toward South Pass's summit, each step carrying them higher into dangerous territory. The air grew thin, making every breath a victory.

Caleb's leg failed him on the steepest slope. The brace snapped with a sound like a breaking twig, sending him stumbling against the wagon wheel. The iron rim finally cracked, proving Fort Laramie's work as worthless as Shaw's promises.

"Thomas!" The name escaped before he could stop it. "Take the reins."

His son's face showed fear beneath determination as he gripped the reins. At seven years old, the trail demanded more than childhood could give.

Emma's patience finally broke. "You're holding them wrong," she snapped, reaching for the reins. "Like this, or you'll kill us all."

"I know what I'm doing!" Thomas jerked away from her grasp. "Just because you write everything down doesn't make you smarter!"

"Both of you, stop." Sarah's voice was weak. Nine days without natural sleep, he had left her hollow. "Thomas, watch Emma's hands. Emma, remember he's doing his best."

The children subsided, but Caleb saw the wound in their eyes. The trail had stolen their childhood games, replacing them with adult fears. Even their quarrels now carried life-or-death weight.

James Davis's steady voice helped to ease the tense mood. "Make camp here. Wheeler's leg needs rest, and Sarah's dead on her feet. South Pass will wait another day."

The wagons circled in the mountain meadow, their shadows stretching long in the evening light. Sarah collapsed onto their wagon bed, finally surrendering to exhaustion. Caleb watched helplessly from his pallet. His leg throbbed with each heartbeat, turning attempts at movement into lessons in pain. The children's voices carried from the outside—Thomas accused Emma of arrogance, and Emma mocked his hunting obsession.

Night fell heavy over South Pass. Sarah slept in a deep sleep of absolute exhaustion while Emma and Thomas took separate watch positions. The other families maintained a camp routine, letting the Wheelers heal in their own time.

Dawn broke clear and was more relaxed. Caleb woke to find Emma studying Thomas's hunting journal, her fingers tracing his careful drawings of animal tracks. Nearby, Thomas bent over Emma's patient notes, sounding out medical terms beneath his breath.

"Your sister sees sickness like you see animal signs," Caleb said quietly. "Different trails, same tracking."

Sarah woke to find them sharing knowledge instead of anger. Her smile carried the first genuine warmth since Rebecca's death as she began teaching both children about medicinal plants. Even Margaret drew closer, though she still wouldn't speak.

The wagon train resumed its climb toward South Pass's summit. Caleb watched his children from the wagon bed.

The sun touched South Pass's highest point as their wagons crested the summit. James Davis pulled his wagon alongside theirs. "Oregon's waiting," he said. "Whenever you're ready."

Caleb nodded, feeling the thin mountain air fill his lungs.

Emma's voice carried from her watch position: "Thomas says we'll have better hunting in the valley."

"Emma's notes say the water will be cleaner there," Thomas added.

The mountain wind caught Margaret's hair as she watched the valley below. Her dress fluttered like a prayer flag, marking their passage into new territory. Behind them, South Pass stood silent.

"Ready?" Caleb asked quietly.

Sarah's hand found his as Emma and Thomas took their positions. Margaret remained silent, but her tiny fingers relaxed their grip on Miss Liberty for the first time since Rebecca's death.

The wagons rolled forward into the descent, leaving South Pass's grief behind.

"Like this." Thomas demonstrated proper rabbit cleaning to Peter Davis, and his movements were sure despite his age. "Keep the meat away from the entrails. Ma says that's how sickness spreads."

The boys worked together hunting and cleaning, providing an escape from the camp's somber air. Their childhood games had turned to survival skills.

"Water's getting low," James Davis reported. "Need to push higher up the slope before dark."

Caleb nodded. "Thomas, take Peter and check the spring.

"The laudanum won't last," she said quietly. "Mother's journal mentioned wild lettuce as a substitute, but I've never prepared it."

"Tell Thomas what to look for. The boy's got sharp eyes."

"Sharp eyes don't help if–" Sarah stopped, her fingers tightening on the medical chest. "If we lose any more."

The unspoken name hung between them: Rebecca Mills, first to fall. They'd lost two more since then – a Davis cousin and Martha Peterson's oldest grandson. The graves stood in a neat row, marking their passage through South Pass's shadow.

Emma's voice carried from the sick wagon, reading aloud to Mary Mills. The girl's fever had broken that morning, but weakness still held her flat. James Mills listened from beyond the rope boundary.

"Pa?" Thomas returned from the spring check, his expression tight. "Water's clean, but we found tracks. Big cat, probably mountain lion."

Caleb contemplated this new threat. "How fresh?"

"This morning, maybe earlier. Peter says they're hunting the same game we are."

Another problem requires a solution. The hunting parties couldn't risk cat attacks but needed meat for strength. Sarah's treatments required clean water, but the spring lay exposed to predators.

Margaret appeared at the wagon door, Miss Liberty hanging limp from one hand. She pointed urgently toward Mary Mills's wagon, where the girl had begun retching again.

"The fever's back," Sarah said, already moving. "Emma, bring the willow bark. Thomas, I need more clean cloths."

Emma measured medicine while Thomas tore strips from their dwindling supply of clean linen. Even Margaret helped silently, carrying water buckets that seemed too large for her tiny hands.

Night fell cold over the wagons. The isolation lanterns provided the needed light as Sarah checked her patients.

"Like animal tracks," Thomas said, studying his sister's notes. "The sickness leaves signs, same as the game."

Emma looked up, surprise softening her exhausted face. "You can read them?"

"Some. See how you marked the fever patterns? Like deer trails showing feeding times."

A cry from the Davis wagon shattered the moment. "Sarah! He's not breathing right!"

The night dissolved into frantic activity. Sarah worked desperately over young Michael Davis, forcing air into fluid-filled lungs. Emma prepared dressings while Thomas ran for more spring water, heedless of mountain lions in the dark.

The mountain stars wheeled overhead, indifferent to human suffering. Sarah fought through the night, but dawn broke gray and final over the Davis wagon. Another small grave would mark their passage through South Pass.

John Morton appeared as they buried Michael Davis. "We're done," he announced, his voice cracking. "My children won't die in these mountains."

Sarah didn't look up from her medical chest. "The journey back's just as dangerous."

"Anything's better than watching them suffer. James, you coming?"

James Mills held Mary's thin hand through the isolation rope. "We've lost too much to turn back now."

The Mortons hitched their wagon as Sarah made them take supplies - medicine, food, and clean water. The parting held no bitterness, only the weight of an impossible choice.

"God go with you," Caleb said quietly.

John Morton touched his hat brim. "And with you. Hope you find your valley."

The wagon disappeared down the mountain slope, leaving three families to continue the climb. Martha Peterson watched them go, her old hands steady on her reins.

"I'm pushing on alone," she announced. "These mountains won't claim any more of mine."

No one argued. Sometimes survival meant separation, each family finding their path through grief.

The evening brought cooler air and fresh challenges. The Davis family's youngest developed a fever while Sarah dozed between patients. Emma handled it capably, her small hands sure as she measured willow bark tea.

"Just like Ma showed us," she whispered to Margaret. "Remember how she helped baby James?"

Margaret didn't respond, but her fingers found Emma's arm and held tight.

As darkness fell, the wagon circle drew closer. Three families remained where five had started, each carrying extra grief but also extra strength. Sometimes, survival meant learning new ways to be whole.

9

DESERT CRUCIBLE

Snake River Country, August 1843

Caleb stood at the Snake River's edge, measuring the water depth with his pole. The river had dropped six feet below normal levels, leaving a steep bank of crumbling mud. Three wagons waited behind him - all that remained of their five-family train.

"Pa." Thomas stepped to his side with his old spyglass. "Shoshoni camp across the river. Three lodges."

Sarah emerged from behind their wagon, wiping her mouth with a shaking hand. Her face held no color, but her voice remained steady. "How's the crossing?"

"Too low." Caleb tested another spot. "The current has channeled to a narrow path. Bank's unstable for the wagons."

Emma consulted her water records, "We've got a quarter of water rations left. We can't wait for the river to rise."

The sun beat against Caleb's neck as he studied the crossing. Their remaining oxen shifted restlessly in the heat, tongues hanging. James Davis checked their leads while his son Peter refilled the drinking buckets.

"There." Caleb marked a spot where the bank sloped gentler. "Current's slower here. We'll double-team the wagons, take them one at a time."

Sarah pressed her hand against the wagon wheel, steadying herself. "The oxen are weak from heat. If we lose any in the crossing-"

"Can't stay here." James Davis joined them. "Snake country's no place for three wagons alone."

Thunder cracked overhead - heat thunder with no promise of rain. The sun had burned away morning clouds, leaving the sky brass-bright and merciless. Sarah disappeared behind the wagon again, and the retching sound carried clearly.

Thomas remained focused on the Shoshoni camp, tracking movement through the glass.

"They're breaking camp," he reported. "Three warriors riding this way."

Caleb tested his leg, finding the usual pain but no weakness. They'd need every able body to manage the crossing. The brake on their wagon had grown unreliable, making steep descents treacherous.

"Emma, check our supplies. Make sure everything's lashed high." He turned to Davis. "James, help me rig double traces. Thomas, keep watch on those riders."

Sarah reappeared, her face composed but her hands trembling slightly as she opened her medical chest. "The laudanum's low. If anyone's hurt in the crossing-"

"We'll manage." Caleb touched her arm briefly. "Check Margaret's water. She's not drinking enough."

Emma's voice carried from the wagon bed: "Water's lower than I calculated. We've got maybe three days at quarter rations."

Thomas lowered the spyglass. "Riders approaching. One's carrying a lance with feathers."

Sarah straightened from checking Margaret. "Peace sign. They're coming to trade."

The morning sun turned the approaching riders into dark silhouettes. Caleb counted weapons automatically—two rifles, one lance, and three knives visible in beaded sheaths. The lead rider raised his hand in greeting as they approached.

"Water signs wrong," the warrior said in careful English. "River drops more by night. Cross now or wait many days."

Caleb studied the man's face - young but weathered. "How long does it take to cross three wagons?"

"Two hours, if oxen strong. Less if we use our ponies to help."

Sarah stepped forward, one hand pressed against her skirt. "We can trade medical supplies for help."

The warrior nodded to his companions. One dismounted, moving to study their wagon arrangements. His practiced eye caught the weak brake, the tired oxen, the signs of extended travel.

"Need six horses." He pointed to places where ropes could be rigged. "Two each wagon. Trade medicine and meat."

The third warrior had noticed Margaret's river drawings. He crouched beside her, adding details with a gentle finger. Margaret watched intently, though she still wouldn't speak.

Emma recorded everything in her journal—measurements, calculations, and the warriors' suggestions. Now, she documented another crisis point in their journey.

"Thomas." Caleb gestured his son closer. "Help Sarah gather trade goods. James, we'll need all hands to rig those traces."

The sun climbed higher as they prepared for the crossing. Sarah's medical supplies bought them six strong ponies and three experienced handlers. The warriors watched their careful preparations with approval.

"Boy reads water well," the lead warrior said, noting Thomas's arrangement of guide ropes. "Sees patterns like our children."

Margaret's drawings had grown more complex, showing currents and depths with strange accuracy. The warrior teaching her nodded in satisfaction, adding marks that looked like trail signs.

Right now, the Snake River demanded their full attention. Its muddy waters held no mercy for weak oxen or failed brakes. They'd cross or fail in the next two hours.

The first ox went down an hour past noon. Its legs buckled beneath the traces as James Davis struggled to guide their strongest team through shin-deep mud. The animal's sides heaved once, then stilled.

"Get the ropes!" Caleb moved as fast as his leg allowed. "Thomas, bring water!"

Thomas ran with the bucket, but the ox's eyes had already glazed. James Davis tried mouth-to-nose breathing like they'd used on foundered horses, but the animal was gone.

"Heat took him." Davis wiped his face. "Too much strain in this weather."

Sarah pressed against the wagon wheel, her face gray. She'd been checking harnesses when the ox fell, and the sudden run through deep mud had cost her. Emma appeared at her mother's elbow with the water dipper.

"Rest," Emma whispered. "I saw you this morning. You need-"

"Not now." Sarah straightened, though her hands shook. "We have to redistribute the weight. That team was our strongest."

The Shoshoni warriors conferred briefly, and then their leader approached. "Use our ponies. No extra charge. Better than losing more oxen."

Caleb studied the dead animals, measuring their chances. Even with the warriors' help, they'd nearly lost their first wagon in the crossing. The river bottom shifted treacherously, and the current ran stronger than it looked.

Thomas worked with Peter Davis to rig new traces for the Indian ponies. "Like this?" Thomas showed his knots to the nearest warrior. "It won't pinch?"

The warrior approved Thomas's work with a nod. He'd introduced himself as Running Creek, and his eyes missed nothing. "Good knots. Strong but quick to cut if needed."

The sun stood directly overhead, burning away the morning's little moisture.

"Three days," Emma reported. "Less, with the extra ponies to water."

Thunder mocked them from the empty sky. The Shoshoni warriors watched their struggle with knowing eyes - they'd seen other wagon trains face the desert's math.

"There is water," Running Creek said finally. "Not here. Two days west. We show you trade for medicine."

A female voice called from across the river. One of the remaining warriors gestured to a woman crossing on horseback - older, her face lined with wisdom.

"White Deer," Running Creek explained. "She knows plants, healing. Sees what others miss."

Sarah swayed slightly as the woman approached. White Deer's sharp eyes caught the movement, and she spoke rapidly to Running Creek.

"She says your wife carries new life," Running Creek translated. "Needs different water than others. We help find."

Caleb turned to Sarah, who pressed one hand to her stomach.

"Four months," she whispered. "I wasn't certain until the sickness started."

"Sarah." Caleb's voice cracked. "Why didn't-"

"Because of this." She gestured to their stuck wagons, the dead ox, and the endless desert. "We can't stop. We can't go back. So I kept working. And I don't think we should tell the children unless necessary."

Caleb nodded in agreement, though hiding his mixed emotions was difficult.

White Deer spoke again, her words carrying gentle authority despite the language barrier. Running Creek translated: "She says desert mothers are strongest. They carry life where others see only death."

The woman dismounted and moved to check Sarah's pulse. Her fingers found pressure points and nodded in satisfaction.

"She will teach you water signs," Running Creek continued. "Secret springs. Plants that hold life. Trade medicine for knowledge."

Caleb's first instinct was refusal—they couldn't spare supplies, trust strangers, or risk their narrow margins. But Sarah's face held too much strain, and the path stretched endlessly ahead.

"What knowledge?" He kept his voice steady.

"Water paths. Safe camps. Plants for the mother." Running Creek pointed west. "Two days to good water if you learn the right signs."

"We'll trade," Caleb said finally. "But we cross these wagons first."

The work continued through the brutal afternoon heat. White Deer mixed something from her medicine pouch for Sarah, easing the sickness enough to let her help. The warriors' ponies proved worth a dozen dead oxen, finding safe paths through treacherous mud.

The sun hung low and red when their last wagon finally crossed. They'd lost one ox but gained something more valuable - knowledge that might keep them alive through the desert's crucible.

Sarah slept in their wagon, White Deer's medicine bringing her the first peace she'd had in weeks. Tomorrow would bring its challenges. But tonight, they rested beside the Snake River, three wagons stronger for knowing their weaknesses.

Dawn did not bring relief from the heat. Running Creek gathered Thomas and Peter Davis as the first light broke the horizon.

"Water signs change in the morning," he explained, checking their water skins. That's the best time to read them."

Thomas buckled his old knife to his belt. "How far?"

"Far as needed." Running Creek studied the boys' preparations. "Plants tell us. Birds tell us. Ground tells us if we listen right."

Caleb watched them prepare from the wagon bed, his leg protesting every movement. The brake repair couldn't wait - their descent into the next valley would kill them with a failed brake.

"I should go with them." He tested his weight on the wrong leg.

"No," Sarah replied. "You're needed here. Thomas knows what to look for."

Emma organized their remaining water supplies while White Deer showed her which containers would preserve it best. The older woman spoke through gesture, teaching Emma to recognize signs of tainted water.

"Heavy things must go," White Deer said through Running Creek's translation. "Water weighs more than memories."

Sarah stared at her mother's China, which had been wrapped carefully since Independence. The desert had already claimed Rebecca's quilt and Martha Peterson's books, and now it demanded more sacrifices.

"The cradle too?" Emma asked softly.

Sarah's hands pressed against her skirts, where new life grew beneath. "We'll build another. In Oregon."

They worked through early morning, redistributing weight as Thomas and the search party disappeared into the desert.

James Davis supervised the unloading, and his trail experience showed in what he chose to keep. "Tools first. Medicine second. Everything else is luxury out here."

The China went first, and each piece was wrapped one final time before being set aside. Sarah's hope chest followed, then James's wedding trunk. The cradle stood alone until last.

White Deer examined Margaret's water drawings, adding marks with his fingers. The girl's sketches grew more detailed as the morning passed, capturing subtle changes in ground color that marked hidden springs.

"Your smallest one sees well," White Deer told Sarah. "Silent watching teaches much."

A cry from the far wagon interrupted them. One of Davis's younger children had found a scorpion in the water barrel.

"Note which barrel," Sarah instructed. "We need to know if others might be contaminated."

The sun climbed higher as they worked. Caleb repaired the brake with James Davis's help, but every movement sent pain shooting through his leg. The modified brace was failing.

"Thomas will find water." Emma's voice carried more certainty than her ten years should allow. "Running Creek knows this land."

Sarah nodded, one hand pressed against her back as she continued sorting. White Deer's medicine had eased the morning sickness, but the heat sapped her strength.

Margaret tugged Sarah's skirt, urgently pointing at her latest drawing. The pattern showed water flowing beneath rock formations similar to those they'd passed yesterday.

White Deer studied the sketch. Her rapid words brought Running Creek's wife to look.

"The child draws old springs," Running Creek's wife explained. "Places our grandmothers knew. Good water, but hidden now."

The day passed with agonizing slowness. They redistributed supplies into every available container, preparing for whatever water Thomas's party found. The abandoned possessions stood in neat rows - physical memories they could no longer afford.

Caleb tested the repaired brake, but his leg buckled on the third try. The pain drove him to his knees as James Davis caught him.

"Rest," Davis said quietly. "Save your strength for when we need it most."

The afternoon heat peaked as Thomas's party appeared on the horizon. They rode slowly, conserving their horses' strength, but Thomas sat straighter than he had that morning.

Running Creek spoke before they entirely stopped. "The boy found water. Good water, deep under stone."

Thomas dismounted. "The water goes underground but doesn't disappear."

He spread a rough map drawn on leather. "Three springs within two days' ride. Running Creek says they'll support the wagons if we're careful."

Sarah studied the water locations while White Deer and Running Creek discussed routes. Emma added the springs to her master map as Thomas explained their findings.

"The ground changes color where water runs deep," he said. "Like Margaret's been drawing."

"Good water for the mother," White Deer said, examining Thomas's map. "Safe camps marked. Better chances now."

They held a council that night, and decisions came quickly - they would abandon their remaining luxuries, convert the space to water storage, and follow Thomas's discovered springs.

"Two weeks to good rivers," Running Creek said. "If you read signs right and travel smart."

The wagon wheel cracked at midday. Caleb heard the sound like breaking bone - sharp and final against desert silence. His leg gave way as he moved to check the damage, sending him hard against sun-heated wood.

"Pa!" Thomas dropped the water bucket, running to help.

"Stay back." Caleb gripped the wagon side, trying to stand. His leg brace shifted, metal scraping metal, then broke completely. "Check the wheel first."

The crack ran deep through seasoned oak. Three spokes hung loose, and the rim had split where it met the hub.

James Davis examined the break while Thomas held the wagon steady. "Can't fix this properly without a forge."

White Deer spoke rapidly to Running Creek, who translated: "Desert wood two days east. Hardwood is good for wheels. But water grows thin."

"Thomas." Caleb's voice cracked as he tried to stand. "You'll need to lead the repair party."

"Yes, sir. Peter can help, and Running Creek knows where-"

"No." James Davis cut in. "Need you here, boy. You're reading water signs better than any of us now. I'll take Peter for the wood."

Margaret tugged Thomas's sleeve, pointing to her latest drawings. She'd mapped a route to deeper water, her tiny fingers tracing paths between rock formations.

Running Creek studied her work. "The silent one sees true. Water runs deep there, where stone meets sand. Enough for two days, maybe three."

The decisions came quickly after that. James Davis would take Peter and two warriors to find wood for the wheel. Thomas would lead the remaining wagons to the water source.

Caleb watched it from the wagon bed, his useless leg propping on their remaining trunk. The broken brace lay beside him, its cumbersome weight absent for the first time since Independence.

Sarah checked Caleb's leg as the repair party rode east. The desert had burned away her midwife's gentleness, leaving efficient movements and careful conservation of resources.

"White Deer knows ways to strengthen the muscle," she said, rewrapping the swollen joint. "Different from Mother's methods, but they work."

They continued toward deeper water throughout the afternoon. Thomas rode ahead with Running Creek, reading signs Cooper had never known to teach.

They reached Margaret's water source as sunset painted the rocks red. The spring ran sweet and cold, hidden beneath stone like Thomas had learned to find.

"Good eye," Running Creek told Margaret. She ducked her head but kept drawing, adding new details to her sketches.

"Different ways to heal," White Deer said, watching Sarah work. "Different ways to survive. All true if you learn to read them."

"Pa?" Thomas paused beside Caleb at the wagon. "I've been thinking about the wheel repair. If we angle the spokes like Shoshoni arrow flights-"

"Show me." Caleb shifted to see his son's drawings in the fading light.

Thomas quickly sketched designs and showed his ideas, which caused Caleb to feel a more incredible pride in his son's abilities.

The stars emerged brilliant against the darkness as the family settled into a familiar routine. Thomas took the first watch with Running Creek while Emma updated her journals. Margaret slept curled beside Sarah.

Caleb lay awake, watching his children adapt and grow stronger. The desert's crucible had burned away his ability to lead, but it forged Thomas into something new—a leader who could read water signs and guide wagons through the wilderness.

Sometimes, survival meant stepping aside and letting strength flow where it would—like the hidden springs Thomas found, the life growing in Sarah's womb, or Margaret's silent wisdom.

Morning brought James Davis's return, the precious wood strapped to tired horses. The Shoshoni warriors had led them to desert ironwood - timber harder than oak and born to survive drought.

Thomas studied the wood grain while White Deer prepared the morning medicines. "See how it grows twisted, Pa? Like it's storing water in the grain."

"Good wood," Running Creek confirmed. "Bends but doesn't break. Like desert people."

They worked through early morning, shaping wood that fought every tool. Caleb supervised from his wagon seat, teaching Thomas the skills his hands could no longer manage.

He instructed, "Angle it like your arrow design. Let the grain support the weight."

Thomas's careful work shaped the wheel. James Davis helped with the heaviest tasks while Peter watched and learned.

Running Creek approved Thomas's design. "Strong joining. Like bow wood backed with sinew. Will hold through hard ground. Time to go," he announced as the wheel settled into place. "Good water waiting north."

White Deer presented Sarah with a medicine pouch - soft leather filled with desert knowledge. The women embraced each other without needing words to share their understanding.

Running Creek gave Thomas a water map drawn on cured hide. "You read signs well now. Trust what the desert tells you."

The parting came with desert simplicity. Thomas led their wagons north, following water signs Running Creek had taught him to read. Each revolution of the new wheel proved the strength of joined knowledge.

"The boy reads water like he was born to it," Running Creek had said at parting. "Some gifts sleep until the desert wakes them."

Caleb watched his son guide them through the wilderness, seeing the leader he'd become. Sometimes, the desert's crucible burned away one kind of strength to forge another.

Sarah's hand found Caleb's as their wagon followed Thomas's lead.

10

MOUNTAIN PRAYER

Blue Mountains, September 1843

The first snowflake hit Caleb's cheek like a warning. He looked up from securing the wagon brake to see dark clouds rolling over the Blue Mountains' jagged peaks. The wind carried the sharp bite of winter, though September had barely begun.

"Pa!" Thomas's voice cracked with urgency. "Cave opening ahead. Big enough for the wagons."

Caleb tested his weight on his bad leg, finding the usual pain amplified by the altitude and cold. The weather had turned faster than any September he'd known, and their three remaining wagons stood exposed on the mountain trail.

Sarah emerged from their wagon, one hand pressed to her stomach while the other gripped the sideboard. Her face was ghostly pale, but she kept her voice steady. "How long to reach the cave?"

"Hour, maybe less." Caleb studied the narrow path. "If the snow holds off."

Emma appeared beside the wheel, clutching her Bible tight. "We should pray first—all of us."

The families gathered quickly as more snowflakes began to fall. James Davis checked his rifle while his wife Catherine helped Mary Mills collect loose supplies. They'd learned to combine prayer with preparation since leaving Independence.

Margaret sat in the wagon doorway, Miss Liberty's cloth face turned toward the storm. She hadn't spoken since Rebecca died in the summer cholera outbreak, but her eyes tracked every snowflake.

Emma's voice rose against the wind as she led their first mountaintop prayer. The words carried authority beyond her ten years, strengthened by months of trial and loss.

"Time to move." James Davis broke the silence as the snow began falling harder. "Thomas, you and Peter guide us to that cave. Rest of us keep the wagons from sliding."

They hitched double teams to each wagon, combining the strength of their remaining oxen. The mountain path had narrowed steadily over the past week, forcing them to navigate areas barely wide enough to accommodate their wheel tracks.

Sarah stumbled as she climbed into their wagon. Caleb caught her arm, feeling the tremor in her muscles. She'd been fighting morning sickness for weeks, though she tried to hide it.

"I'm fine," she said before he could speak. "The altitude, nothing more."

But they both knew the truth she hadn't voiced. The timing matched her previous pregnancies.

The wagons moved slowly through thickening snow. Thomas and Peter walked ahead, marking safe passage.

As they reached the cave mouth, the storm struck full force. The wind drove snow sideways, and the temperature plummeted. James Davis directed them to form a windbreak with the wagons while Caleb examined the cave's depth.

"Room enough," he reported. "If we pack tight."

They worked quickly to transfer supplies into the cave's shelter. Sarah coordinated medical stores while Mary Mills organized food supplies. The children gathered wood before the snow could soak it thoroughly.

Caleb's leg gave out as he helped secure the last wagon. The pain shot from hip to ankle, dropping him against the wheel. Thomas reached him first, offering the same shoulder that had steadied him since Fort Laramie.

"Rest, Pa," Thomas said. "Davis and I can finish."

The cave interior slowly transformed into a temporary sanctuary. Sarah hung canvas to partition sleeping spaces, and the Mills family shared their remaining coffee.

Night fell early, and they were trapped in mountain stone and a winter storm. They gathered around small fires, careful with precious fuel.

Sarah's collapse came during morning prayers. One moment, she stood beside Caleb; the next, she crumpled without warning. Emma caught her before she hit the stone, her small hands surprisingly strong.

"Ma?" Emma's voice carried knowledge beyond her years. "Is it like with James?"

The cave fell silent except for the wind. Sarah's fingers pressed against her skirt, no longer hiding what they'd all suspected.

Thomas hunched at the cave's mouth; his lips pressed closed with recollection. "Winter's coming early. The baby..."

"Will have God's protection," Emma cut in. She opened her Bible to marked passages. "Like Moses in the desert."

Margaret crossed the cave with small, specific steps. Her tiny hand found Sarah's belly, pressing gently against the new life. Their youngest hadn't touched anyone voluntarily since Rebecca died.

The elk herd's arrival interrupted the morning's events. Thomas spotted them first—a dozen animals moving below the cave mouth, forced down the mountain by early snow.

"We need that meat." James Davis checked his rifle. "Won't last long at this altitude."

Caleb gripped his crutches. "I'm going."

"Pa, no." Thomas stepped between him and the cave mouth. "Your leg-"

"Will hurt either way." Caleb kept his voice firm. "You'll need every rifle."

The mountain air cut like knives as they followed the elk tracks. Snow had drifted knee-deep in places, making every step an act of will. Caleb's leg screamed with each movement, but he forced himself forward.

The shot came faster than any of them expected. One moment, the elk stood at the edge of a small clearing. The next, Caleb's rifle cracked with thunder force.

The animal dropped instantly - a clean kill at an impossible range. In amazement, Thomas stared at his father as James Davis wielded his blade to begin butchering.

When they returned, Margaret saw them first. She stood in the cave mouth despite the cold. As Caleb limped into view, her tiny voice broke months of silence.

"Papa hurt?"

The words cracked the mountain's winter spell. Sarah's medicine kit clattered against the stone as she moved forward. Emma embraced Margaret fiercely while Thomas steadied their father's final steps.

The cave vibrated with celebration as James Davis distributed fresh meat and Emma led prayers of thanksgiving.

Thomas demonstrated the hunt's events for younger children, his voice describing the details of his father's shot. Margaret spoke in short phrases, each word a victory against summer's grief.

Night brought its healing. While Emma organized prayer rotations, Sarah treated Caleb's leg with White Deer's medicines. Thomas and James Davis worked to preserve the meat for the journey ahead.

"Trail's clearing," Thomas reported from his morning scout. "Valley visible below."

James Davis nodded approval. "Two days' decent with good weather. Need to start while the snow's frozen."

Margaret named the baby while they packed the altar away. "James," she said with certainty. "For angels watching."

Sarah's hand found her belly as Caleb watched their preparations. The mountain had demanded its price in pain and fear, but it gave strange gifts in return - Margaret's voice, Sarah's revelation, and faith forged stronger than winter stone.

The descent consumed their third day on the hill. Caleb watched from the wagon seat as Thomas and Peter worked ahead through the treacherous snow. The boys moved with the confidence of veteran scouts now.

"The baby's moving." Sarah's voice carried quiet wonder as she checked their medical supplies. Her fingers lingered on her mother's journal, touching her careful notes about winter births.

Emma looked up from her writing. "Does it feel like before? Like with–"

"Different." Sarah cut her off gently. "Each child brings their signs."

The wagon wheel struck ice, sending them lurching toward the cliff edge. Caleb grabbed the brake lever as Thomas and Peter rushed to help. Pain shot through his leg, but he held firm until it stabilized.

"Need to chain the wheels," James Davis called behind them. "Snow's getting soft."

They worked quickly to wrap iron chains around each wheel. The links bit into frozen ruts, providing a grip against the slippery ice.

"Found deer tracks," Peter reported as they finished. "Fresh ones, heading toward that grove."

Caleb tested his leg, finding pain but no weakness. "How far?"

"Half a mile, maybe less." Peter glanced at Thomas. "We could–"

"No." James Davis's voice carried authority earned through months of crisis. "Storm's building again. Make camp while we can."

The weather proved him right within the hour. Snow fell in thick curtains as they formed a tight wagon circle.

"God provides shelter," Emma read from their Bible. Her voice stayed steady despite the wind's howl. "Even in the wilderness, His hand guides us."

Margaret touched Sarah's belly again, her small face serious. "Baby James cold?"

"No, sweet one." Sarah gathered her close. "The baby's warm, just like you were."

They slept crowded together that night, sharing body heat. Thomas took the first watch with Peter, their rifles ready against mountain predators. Caleb lay awake, listening to his family breathe while snow piled against the wagon walls.

Dawn brought another challenge. As they prepared to move, the brake rope snapped, nearly sending their wagon into the Davis family's rig. Thomas caught the lead oxen's harness while Caleb fought the brake lever.

"Emma!" Sarah's voice cracked with urgency. "Get my sewing kit. The heavy thread."

They worked together to splice the rope, combining Sarah's stitching with Caleb's knots.

Margaret watched from the wagon door. Her voice came stronger now, though she spoke only of babies and angels.

"God watching," she announced as they finished, " like with Moses."

Their progress down the slope continued through the day. James Davis led while Thomas and Peter scouted ahead. Despite his leg's protest, Caleb kept their wagon steady.

"There." Thomas's voice carried sharp with excitement near sunset. "Green trees below the snow line."

They stopped to study the valley stretched below them. Pine forests marked where winter's grip faded, promising game and shelter after the mountain's barren stone.

Their path narrowed to bare wagon width, its surface slick with frozen snow. Caleb tested the ground with his crutch, finding treacherous ice beneath white powder.

"Can't risk the wagons here." James Davis studied the trail ahead. "Need to double-check every foot."

"Baby James wants down," Margaret announced, one hand pressed against Sarah's skirt. "Like Moses in rushes."

"Not yet, sweet one." Sarah's voice held forced lightness. "The baby needs to wait for spring flowers."

They moved with aching slowness, checking each yard of ground. Caleb kept the brake ready, his leg screaming as he balanced between pain and necessity. The wagon wheels left deep ruts in fresh snow, marking their passage.

Emma organized the children into work groups, gathering fallen pine boughs for traction. "Like Israel coming to the promised land," she said as they worked. "Through wilderness and water."

"And snow," Thomas added, marking another dangerous patch. "Don't remember Moses dealing with ice."

"Storm coming." Peter's warning cut through their work. "Big one, from the north."

Caleb studied the clouds gathering over distant peaks. The temperature had dropped steadily since dawn.

"Two hours, maybe less." James Davis checked their position. "Ridge ahead might give shelter."

Sarah's collapsed again without warning. One moment, she stood checking supplies; the next, she crumpled against the wagon wheel. Emma was walking beside her and was able to catch her.

"The baby?" Caleb fought his crutches, trying to reach them.

"Altitude." Sarah's voice came thin with effort. "Just need to rest."

But they all heard the fear behind her words. The mountain air grew thinner as they climbed, stealing strength from mother and unborn child.

James Davis made the hard decision. "We rest here. Storm or no storm."

They formed a tight circle with the wagons, using pine boughs to block wind between the gaps.

Thomas returned from his final scout, snow crusting his coat. "Ridge is too far. Storm's moving faster than we can."

They battened down as the mountain winds struck. Canvas snapped like rifle shots while snow drove horizontally against the wagon walls. The temperature plummeted, turning water into ice in the barrels.

Sarah fought another wave of sickness as Caleb helped her arrange their blankets. Her hand pressed against her belly, protecting the new life growing there.

"I can't lose another one," she whispered. "Not up here. Not like James."

"You won't." Emma's voice came fierce with faith. She opened her Bible to marked passages about mercy and protection. "God didn't bring us this far to leave us."

James Davis organized the men into watch rotations while Mary Mills distributed precious coffee. They'd learned to combine practical preparation with spiritual comfort, knowing both were needed for survival.

The storm raged through early afternoon. Sarah slept fitfully while Emma read scripture and Margaret sang. Thomas helped Peter check wagon lashings, their shoulders pressed against the winter wind.

Caleb watched from their wagon door, measuring the storm's fury against their supplies. His leg ached with familiar pain, but something else hurt deeper – the fear of losing another child to forces beyond his control.

The break came near sunset. One moment, snow drove against the canvas; the next, silence. They emerged to find the world transformed – white perfection stretched endless under clearing skies.

Thomas and Peter returned from checking the trail ahead. Their faces carried hope tempered by experience.

"Path's clear to the ridge," Thomas reported. "Snow packed hard enough to hold the wagons."

The wagons rolled forward as sunset painted snow to gold. They moved steadily, following tracks that God or angels had preserved through the storm.

Night caught them halfway to the ridge. The temperature dropped sharply and fast, turning Thomas's breath to ice and freezing the wagon grease solid. Caleb helped Thomas check their wheels while James Davis organized the evening camp.

"Something's moving up there," Peter's voice cut through the darkness. "It was near the tree line."

Thomas raised the old spyglass, searching the shadows. "Wolves, maybe. Following the elk down."

They doubled the watch that night. James Davis took the first rotation with Peter while Thomas cleaned his rifle beside their fire. The weapon had grown worn by months of hard use.

"Should have traded for a new one at Fort Laramie," Thomas said, checking the barrel's rifling.

"Some things worth keeping." Caleb touched their family Bible, its leather worn smooth by generations of hands. "They carry memories in their scars."

"The baby's restless tonight." Sarah's voice carried quiet concern. "Moving more than usual."

The cold air was heavy as dawn broke across the ridge. Caleb tested his leg and found fresh joint pain; the altitude had stiffened. The wagon's brake lever had frozen solid, requiring Thomas and Peter's combined strength to break free.

"Path looks clear ahead." James Davis studied the trail through the spyglass. "Valley's closer now. Might make timber by nightfall."

They moved with careful haste, watching for ice beneath the snow. The wagons rolled steadily despite frozen grease.

The wolves appeared just past noon. Three gray shapes moved parallel to their wagon track, following with patient hunger. Thomas raised his rifle while Peter signaled a warning to the other wagons.

"Won't attack while we're moving." James Davis kept his voice steady. "But keep the children close."

The temperature dropped again as afternoon shadows lengthened. Caleb felt the change in his leg first - a deep ache that warned of danger ahead. The wagon wheels began to slip more frequently, fighting snow that had turned treacherous with cold.

"Ice storm coming." Thomas pointed to clouds building behind them. "Like the one that caught the Kendricks in June."

"We'll need more firewood." James Davis studied their dwindling supply. "Won't last another cold night."

Thomas stepped forward, rifle ready. "Peter and I can–"

"No." Caleb cut him off. "Not with wolves watching. We burn wagon boards if we have to."

The ice arrived with sunset, coating everything in a frozen blanket. The wagons formed a tight circle, using every scrap of canvas to block wind between gaps. The wolves' howls were unmistakable now.

Caleb kept watch with James Davis, measuring wolf howls against distance and darkness. The break came near midnight. Thunder cracked across the ridge, bringing rain instead of snow. The wolves' howls faded as lightning turned night to brief day.

Sarah stood in their wagon door, watching lightning paint the valley below.

"The baby's quiet now," she said softly. "Sleeping through the storm."

Morning broke with an unexpected warmth. The rain had washed away most of the snow, leaving the trail muddy but passable. Caleb watched Thomas and Peter check and mark the path ahead. "Valley's closer than we thought," James Davis lowered the glass. "We might reach timber by sunset if we push."

Sarah emerged from their wagon, her movements stronger after the night's rest. The mountain air had painted color in her cheeks, replacing yesterday's gray exhaustion.

"The baby's strong this morning," she said quietly to Caleb. "Like he knows we're almost down."

They moved steadily downslope, following tracks the thaw had exposed. The wagons rolled easier now, their wheels finding purchase in mud rather than ice. Even the brake held firm, though Caleb kept ready for trouble.

Thomas spotted the elk herd near noon. Six animals moved below them, heading toward distant timber. James Davis raised his rifle, but the shot would alert any wolves still watching.

"We've got enough dried meat," Sarah said. "Better to travel quietly and fast."

The wisdom proved sound when Peter spotted fresh wolf tracks crossing their path. The prints led toward the elk herd, drawing the predators away from their wagons.

"Pa?" Thomas paused in his work. "Think we'll reach timber before dark?"

"God willing." Caleb tested his leg, finding pain but less stiffness. "If the trail holds."

The afternoon brought their first glimpse of pine trees untouched by snow. The sight raised everyone's spirits.

"Different from James's time," Sarah said softly to Caleb. "This feels right like the baby knows his path."

They reached the first stand of pines as sunset painted the mountain gold. The wagons rolled from mud onto soft needles, their wheels finally turning quiet after days of frozen ground.

"Like coming home," Mary Mills said as she helped Sarah prepare dinner. "Been so long since we smelled pine."

They slept easier that night, wrapped in pine scent and renewed hope. The mountain stood white against stars, but its power felt distant now.

11

THE FINAL CHOICE

The Dalles, Oregon Territory, October 1843

The first gray light crept over The Dalles as Caleb leaned against their wagon. His fingers found another crack in the troublesome iron rim—metal stressed beyond repair. Sarah's retching carried from behind the wagon, each sound striking like physical pain.

"The morning sickness is worse." Emma's voice stayed low as she checked their water barrel. "We've got half rations left. Maybe less."

Caleb nodded. Their animals stood motionless in the pre-dawn chill, heads hanging. Even Thomas's gentle coaxing couldn't convince the lead ox to move.

"Pa." Thomas appeared beside the wheel, the old spyglass clutched tight. "Riverboats are loading. James Davis says they're charging thirty dollars gold per wagon."

Sarah emerged from behind the wagon, wiping her mouth with a shaking hand. The months of pregnancy had carved deep shadows beneath her eyes. She held one hand supporting the baby, the other steadying herself on the sideboard.

"How far to the Lolo Pass crossing?" she asked.

"Two days." Caleb tested their brake, finding more wear. "If the weather holds."

Emma consulted her journal. "We've got supplies for four days at quarter rations. Less if the snow starts."

The trading post cast a long shadow as the sun cleared the horizon. Other wagons crowded the riverbank, their owners haggling with stone-faced boatmen. James Davis's voice carried across the morning air as he argued prices.

"Mary says the last boat lost two wagons. But the Lolo Pass took four families in the mountain snow." Thomas said, expressing concern.

"We need to know more." Caleb checked the wagon's weakened axle. "Thomas, see what you can learn about the animals' chances on either route. Emma, find out what supplies we can trade."

The children completed their assignments, and Thomas paused only to help Emma store her journal.

James Davis approached as Sarah retreated into the wagon. His rifle hung ready across his back, trail dust ground permanent into his coat.

"River's running high," he reported. "Boats won't bargain below twenty-five gold. Lolo Pass's already seen snow."

Caleb absorbed this against their dwindling options. The wagon's axle groaned as he shifted his weight, metal stressed beyond safe limits.

"How's Mary holding up?"

"Scared of the water." Davis's voice held careful neutrality. "But more scared of mountain snow. Sarah needs proper shelter before that baby comes."

The trading post bell marked morning hour as wagons crowded the river dock. Each family faced the same choice—specific expenses against uncertain survival. The mountain passes loomed white and final against the October sky.

The axle's final crack came with a sound like breaking hope.

The wagon listed sharply right as the metal gave way, sending tools scattering across the frozen ground. Thomas reached the brake first, his hands fighting the lever as Emma scrambled to catch falling supplies.

"Sarah!" Caleb fought toward the wagon bed. "Hold on!"

His wife's cry of pain cut through the morning air. She clutched the sideboard as the wagon tilted, her other hand pressed against her belly.

James Davis appeared with support poles while Thomas steadied the animals. The boy's voice stayed calm as he gentled the frightened oxen.

"The supplies—" Sarah tried to stand but doubled over instead.

"Stay still." Emma's voice carried quiet authority. "Thomas and I will handle it."

Caleb touched the wagon's broken axle, feeling the death of another dream beneath his fingers. Sometimes survival meant learning what to surrender—and when letting go meant holding on to something more precious.

Thunder rolled across the mountain peaks as the first real snow fell.

The trading post's lantern cast sharp shadows as the family gathered for council. Sarah sat propped against their remaining possessions, one hand pressed constantly against her dress. Emma had arranged what they could carry in careful piles while Thomas secured the animals close.

"The river boats won't wait." James Davis called again. "Storm's pushing them out by morning."

"And the Lolo Pass?" Caleb kept his voice steady for the children.

"Already snowbound past the first ridge. But the Mills wagon made it through last week. Trail's marked if you know where to look."

Margaret sat between her parents as she watched the snow pile against the broken wagon. Her tiny voice carried clear in the lantern light: "No boats, Papa. Angels don't like water."

"We can't afford river passage." Emma consulted her journal. "Not with what's left after Fort Laramie."

Thomas spoke from where he had checked the animals. "The oxen won't cross water now. They're too tired, too scared. But they know mountain trails."

Caleb absorbed their words against the sound of snow hitting the canvas. They'd lost tools at Fort Laramie, friends to summer fever, and now their wagon to mountain trails. Each sacrifice marked their passage west.

"We'll need to leave most everything." Sarah's voice strengthened as she planned. Just what we can carry or load on the animals."

Emma worked diligently, calculating bare minimums. "Medical supplies first. Then food, warm clothes, and—"

"The family Bible." Sarah cut in. "Some things weigh more in memory than pounds."

James Davis stood, decision clear in his stance. "We'll take the river. Mary can't face mountain snow, not after last winter. But I'll mark the trail clear before we launch."

The families parted as the storm grew more assertive. Davis and his children would ride the river while the Wheelers walked the mountain.

Snow fell harder as they sorted their remaining possessions. The broken wagon stood sentinel, marking another ending on their trail west. But Sarah's hand stayed steady on her medical chest, and Thomas confidently led their animals.

Dawn broke gray and final as they prepared to move. Thomas had redistributed supplies across their remaining animals, using knots learned from Shoshoni teachers. Emma supported Sarah while Margaret walked between them.

The riverboats disappeared around the bend, carrying James Davis's family toward Oregon's heart. Caleb watched them go, measuring friendship against necessity. Sometimes, survival meant walking different paths.

Snow fell steadily now, marking their way up Lolo Pass. They carried what mattered most—Sarah's medical chest, Emma's journals, Thomas's confidence, and Margaret's quiet faith. The broken wagon stood behind them, its wheels marking one more sacrifice to Western dreams.

The silence held something like a prayer as they took their first steps up Lolo Pass.

Night fell bitter cold across their meager camp. Thomas had found a sheltered spot beneath towering pines where Sarah could rest against storm-bare rock.

"The baby's quiet now." Sarah's voice carried exhausted relief. "The willow bark helps."

Caleb checked their animals, ensuring Thomas's knots held firm. The boy had learned his lessons well—each load balanced perfectly.

The storm raged through the darkness while the Wheeler family slept fitfully beneath shared blankets. Tomorrow would bring fresh challenges, but tonight, they rested, knowing they'd chosen right.

12

WALKING IN WINTER

Final Stretch of Lolo Pass, October 1843

The morning darkness pressed against Caleb's eyelids as he watched Emma scrape the last ice from their cooking pot. Beside him, Sarah's breathing carried the tight control of hidden pain.

"Water's ready, Ma." Emma's voice stayed steady despite the cold. "I saved the pine needles for a second brewing."

Thomas appeared through the pre-dawn shadows, snow crusting his coat. "Lead ox isn't eating." His words formed white clouds in the frozen air. "Might need to redistribute the load again."

Caleb pushed against his walking staff, forcing stiff joints to move. His leg burned with familiar fire as he stood, but he kept his voice even. "How much feed left?"

"Three days at half rations." Emma consulted her notebook without being asked. "Less if the snow gets deeper."

Sarah straightened from her bedroll, one hand pressed against her swollen belly. "I can walk today," she said, but her fingers trembled as she reached for Emma's help.

"You'll rest." Caleb kept his tone firm. "Thomas, check those travois lashings before we move."

The sun crept above the eastern mountains as Emma divided their morning food. Quarter portions had become standard since losing the wagon, but she stretched them with trail wisdom beyond her ten years.

"Pine bark helps fill empty spaces," she said, passing Caleb his share. "The Shoshoni women showed me how to prepare it."

Sarah managed three bites before the morning sickness took hold. She disappeared behind a snow-laden pine, Emma following with the last of their willow bark tea.

Caleb watched Thomas adjust the travois rigging, and the boy's movements were sure.

"Pa?" Thomas tested a leather strap. "Think we'll make the settlement soon?"

"God willing." Caleb pulled their family Bible from its oilcloth wrapping. "Four days to the valley if the weather holds."

"Six days of food." Emma had returned, her calculations precise. "If we stretch the beans with snow."

The lead ox's collapse came without warning. One moment, the animal stood steady in his traces; the next, his legs buckled beneath him. "He's cold straight through." Thomas's voice cracked. "Emma, I need your blanket. Now."

Emma didn't hesitate. She unwrapped her spare blanket from their supplies, the wool already moving toward the fallen ox before Caleb could object.

"He's dying." Sarah's medical knowledge carried even here. "Thomas, remember what Standing Bear taught about clean kills."

But Thomas pressed his face against the ox's neck, his shoulders shaking. "Just tired. He needs rest."

Margaret's tiny voice broke the morning silence. "His name is Brave." She touched the ox's nose with gentle fingers. "Angels know brave ones."

They worked through early morning, trying to save the animal that had pulled their wagon since Independence. Sarah watched from her makeshift bed, one hand pressed against her belly as another contraction passed. The pains had grown stronger since leaving the wagon, though she tried to hide them. The ox died as the sun reached full height. Thomas stood straight-backed as James Davis had taught him, accepting the loss like the man he was becoming.

"We need to redistribute the weight." Caleb kept his voice steady for his son's sake. "Emma, check what we can leave. Thomas, help me with these traces."

They repacked their remaining supplies while Margaret sang hymns to the fallen ox. Sarah's medical chest rode highest now, protecting precious medicines against the snow.

The day wore endless as they pushed forward. Sarah's pain grew worse with each step, though she forced herself to keep moving.

"Rest." Caleb caught her arm as she stumbled. "Emma, help your mother. Thomas, find us shelter before dark."

Thomas disappeared into the snow with his old spyglass. The boy's tracking skills had grown through necessity, each crisis adding to his knowledge.

"The baby's restless." Sarah's voice stayed quiet, meant for Caleb alone. "Moving more than James did."

Emma prepared their evening camp. Margaret gathered dry moss for their fire, her small shape bright against the snow. The cave Thomas found near sunset probably saved their lives. Its entrance faced away from the wind, and dry wood lay scattered inside.

"Cooper mentioned caves like this." Thomas's pride showed through his exhaustion. "Said trappers use them during winter storms."

They crowded inside as darkness fell, sharing body heat and remaining blankets. Sarah's pains eased somewhat, though Emma kept careful watch.

"Like the stable in Bethlehem." Margaret's voice carried clear in the firelit space. "Maybe Jesus will visit our cave."

Emma opened their family Bible, the firelight catching its worn pages. "Each step's a prayer," she read, " each mile a psalm."

Thomas took the first watch. "The animals trust us to lead them home," he said, checking his guide ropes. "We can't fail them."

The night passed in a series of small victories. Their fire stayed lit, the medicines remained unfrozen, and Sarah managed some sleep between contractions.

Caleb watched his family through the midnight hour. Emma's strength kept them fed, Thomas's leadership found shelter, and Margaret's faith lit their darkness.

Dawn crept gray and grudging across their cave mouth. Emma stretched from her watch position, "Three cups of beans." She kept her voice low as Sarah slept. "Half-pound of dried meat. Tea leaves almost gone."

Thomas appeared from his dawn check, snow crusting his coat. "Found rabbit tracks. Fresh ones. If Cooper's snares still work-"

"No." Caleb tested his leg, finding fresh pain but no weakness. "Storm's building. We stay together today."

"The settlement can't be more than four days ahead." She tried to rise, but Emma's hand on her shoulder kept her down. "If we stretch the supplies-"

"You'll rest." Emma's voice carried quiet authority. "Thomas found pine bark yesterday. I can make it stretch."

The morning passed in careful conservation. Emma brewed pine needle tea while Thomas checked their remaining animals. Two oxen stood steady in the snow, their breath forming white clouds in the frozen air.

"Need to move them more." Thomas tested each animal's legs. "Keep the blood flowing. Snow's getting deeper."

Sarah managed half a cup of tea before the sickness took hold. Emma held her mother's shoulders as the precious liquid came back up.

"The baby doesn't like pine bark." Sarah tried to smile. "Your brother James was the same way."

Caleb marked their remaining distance on the old map. The settlement lay somewhere ahead, but winter snow had erased familiar landmarks.

"We follow the river valley." He traced their route for Thomas's benefit. "Two days to lower ground if we're reading the signs right."

The storm struck as they broke camp. The wind drove snow horizontally, stealing their breath and direction. Thomas led their oxen through deepening drifts while Emma helped Sarah manage the cold.

"Need to turn back." Caleb fought to see through white darkness. "That cave-"

"No." Sarah's voice carried steel beneath exhaustion. "Storm might last days. We'll freeze or starve if we wait."

"Angels leave footprints," Margaret said with confidence. "Show us the way home."

They pushed forward through the morning. Emma's careful rationing would be in vain if the storm held them too long.

"River's close," Thomas called back through the wind. "Can hear it under the ice."

Sarah stumbled near midday, her strength finally giving out. Caleb caught her before she fell, feeling the heat of fever beneath her coat.

"Make camp." His voice cracked with command. "Emma, find shelter. Thomas, secure the animals."

They huddled beneath a snow-laden pine as Emma constructed a makeshift windbreak, turning blankets and branches into temporary walls.

"Last of the willow bark." She measured the medicine. "But the fever's not high yet."

Night fell bitterly cold across their shelter. Emma divided their last beans while Thomas maintained a desperate fire. "Tell us about Oregon, Pa." Thomas's voice carried through the darkness. "About our valley at the end."

Caleb measured hope against reality before speaking. "Green trees tall as churches. Rich soil that's never known a plow. Rivers running clear as day."

"With a proper house," Emma added. "Big enough for the baby's cradle."

"And angels." Margaret's faith ran bone-deep. "Waiting to show us home."

Sarah woke as midnight passed. Her fever was broken, but her strength drained. "How far?" The question carried all their fears.

"Close." Caleb kept his voice steady. "The settlement's close now."

Thomas took the last watch, his small shape dark against their failing fire. "The oxen trust us," he whispered to the night. "We can't fail them now."

Dawn came across their makeshift camp. They carefully divided their food by Emma's measure, each portion representing another step toward distant hope.

The storm had passed, leaving knee-deep snow and a brutally clear sky. Emma spotted the smoke first. Her hands froze mid-count over their last beans as she stared westward.

"There." She pointed toward distant mountains. "Above the tree line."

Thomas raised his spyglass, his hands steady despite the cold. "Settlement fires." His voice cracked with hope. "Has to be. Indians burn different wood."

"How far?" Caleb studied the distance through the glass.

"Two days," Thomas replied. "Maybe less if the snow holds firm."

Margaret stood in their broken trail. Her tiny voice carried clear in the frozen air: "Angels burn bright fires."

They moved with purpose through the afternoon. Emma stretched their last food into something close to a meal while Thomas led their oxen across broken ground.

"The settlement will have medicines." Sarah's voice stayed quiet. It was meant for Caleb alone. "For the baby, when it's time."

Caleb checked their remaining supplies as darkness threatened. Emma's careful rationing had kept them alive since they had lost the wagon, but arithmetic couldn't create food from empty bags.

"Snow's getting deeper," Thomas called back through the gathering dark. "Need to find shelter before full night."

Margaret walked beside their last ox, her tiny hand resting on its shoulder. The animal followed her touch like salvation, each step matching her own.

"Tell us about the settlement, Pa." Thomas's voice carried across their meager fire. "What Cooper told you."

"Solid walls." Caleb fed another precious branch to the flames. "Enough food stored for winter. A proper doctor for your mother."

Sarah's breath caught on another contraction, but her voice stayed steady. "With a garden come spring. Room for the baby to grow strong."

"And a school," Emma added. "Books like we had in Pennsylvania."

"Jesus loves gardens," Margaret added. "Angels plant flowers for Him."

Dawn broke mercilessly. They shouldered their remaining supplies as Thomas led the oxen through fresh snow.

Emma's notebook held their last inventory: a half-cup of beans, three pieces of dried meat, and a handful of pine bark. Her careful measurements couldn't stretch anything into survival.

Sarah's pain grew worse with each step, though she forced herself forward. The baby moved restlessly, fighting against the cold like its mother.

Thomas had frozen mid-step, his spyglass pressed to his eye. "Bells, " his voice shook. I can see the church bells."

The sound carried thin and precious across the frozen distance—settlement bells marking morning prayer. Hope rang against desperation as their last strength caught fire.

Margaret reached the top of the final ridge first. Her tiny voice cracked with joy as she saw the settlement spread below.

Sarah's legs gave out at the sight. Emma caught her mother before she fell, supporting her weight as they studied their journey's end.

Wooden walls rose strong against winter's grip. Smoke curled from stone chimneys while livestock moved in sheltered yards. The church bell rang again, calling faithful to morning prayers.

Thomas led their oxen down the last slope, his shoulders straight with pride. Cooper's lessons had carried them true -- each step measured against survival's demands.

Caleb lifted Margaret as they approached the settlement gate. His leg burned with familiar fire, but hope drove him forward.

The guard's challenge came sharp with suspicion: "Who comes?"

"Wheeler family." Caleb kept his voice steady. "From Pennsylvania by way of Independence."

The gate swung wide as Sarah's last strength failed. Emma supported her mother while Thomas guided their oxen through.

Margaret's tiny hand pulled the church bell rope as they entered. The sound carried across the morning air, marking the journey's end.

They'd walked through winter's crucible, carrying hope and fear equally. The settlement offered sanctuary, but survival had forged something stronger than sanctuary could provide.

The bell's final note hung crystalline in frozen air as the gate closed behind them. They'd reached their valley's edge, carried by Emma's careful rationing, Thomas's sure leadership, Sarah's desperate strength, and Margaret's unshakeable faith.

The settlement church's warmth hit the family like an embrace from a long-missed friend. Rough-hewn pews held two dozen settlers - more people than they'd seen since The Dalles. Sarah's fingers dug into Emma's shoulder as another contraction passed.

"Doctor's away." The preacher's wife approached, her eyes measuring Sarah's condition. "Midwife Peterson might help. She came through last month."

"Ma needs rest first, " Emma said with quiet authority. "A warm place, if you can spare it."

Thomas appeared from settling the oxen, snow melting from his coat. "Animals are fed. Mr. Harrison says we can use the old Cooper cabin."

"Samuel Cooper's place?" Caleb shifted Margaret's weight. "He made it through?"

"Two weeks ago." The preacher's wife led them toward the cabin. "Left good word for any Wheeler following."

The cabin stood empty but solid, with a stone fireplace in one room. Sarah sank onto a wooden bench as Emma checked the chimney draw.

"Thomas, we need water." Emma unloaded their last supplies. "Margaret can help gather kindling."

Thomas returned with a water bucket as Sarah fought another contraction. Her face had gone gray with effort.

"The baby's too active." She pressed both hands against her belly. "Coming too soon."

Emma measured their remaining willow bark. "We've got medicine for three days. Thomas can check if the settlement has more."

Caleb caught his son's arm as Thomas headed for the door. "Take Cooper's glass back first. Show them we keep our promises."

The spyglass's brass caught firelight as Thomas wrapped it carefully. Cooper's last gift had guided them true - each step marked against winter's demands.

"The settlement has food stores." Emma consulted her notebook. "If we can trade work-"

"Cooper left credit." The preacher's wife reappeared with blankets. "Said any Wheeler could draw against his account."

Sarah's breath hitched as another pain hit. The baby moved restlessly, fighting October's grip like its mother.

Margaret laid fresh kindling as Emma banked their first proper fire since leaving the wagon. The flames caught quickly, warming the cabin's ancient walls.

Midwife Peterson arrived at sunset, and her lined face held welcome familiarity - they'd crossed paths at Fort Laramie.

"Catherine Barrett's girl." She set her medicine chest down. "Your mother taught me birthing fever cures in '32."

Sarah managed a weak smile. "She said you had steady hands."

"Steady enough." The midwife checked Sarah's pulse. "This little one's eager to see Oregon."

Emma unpacked and stored their belongings while Thomas carried water. Each item found its place—the medicine chest riding highest, the family Bible protected from dampness.

Margaret sat beside her mother, her tiny fingers tracing patterns on Sarah's sleeve.

Night settled heavily across the settlement. Emma divided their first full meal since leaving the wagon while Thomas tended the animals.

"Cooper marked this cabin for us." Caleb studied the solid walls. "Said we'd need shelter before spring."

Sarah's hands pressed against another contraction. "He knew about the baby?"

"Knew about you." Caleb kept his voice steady. "Said Catherine Barrett's daughter would need proper walls for winter birthing."

Emma sorted through Midwife Peterson's herbs, her fingers sure on each packet. "Like Grandmother's journal showed us. Everything we need."

Thomas returned from final animal checks, his shoulders straight with pride. "Oxen are settled. Found good hay in the barn."

Caleb watched his family settle into their first natural shelter since The Dalles. Emma's careful preparation had kept them alive. Thomas's leadership had guided them true. Sarah's strength had carried them forward. Margaret's faith had lit their way.

Their journey wasn't over – the baby would come too soon, winter held three months yet, and spring lay distant.

At dawn, Caleb woke to find Sarah shivering despite the blankets and fire. Her skin burned beneath his touch.

"Birthing fever." Midwife Peterson's voice carried grim knowledge. "Same as your mother fought in '32."

Emma was already moving, her hands steady on the medicine chest. "Grandmother's journal mentions wild lettuce tea. If Thomas can find it-"

"No plants in October snow." The midwife checked Sarah's pulse. "But the settlement has other remedies."

Thomas appeared from tending the oxen, ice crusting his coat. "Settlement store's open. Cooper's credit still holds."

"Check what medicines they have." Caleb forced his leg to move. "Emma knows the names from her journal."

Margaret sat beside Sarah. Her tiny fingers stroked her mother's hair as she sang fragments of hymns.

The fever rose throughout the morning. Emma worked with Midwife Peterson while Thomas traded Cooper's good name for supplies. Each trip brought back less than they needed.

"Settlement's low on everything." Thomas set down three precious willow bark packets. "The storm's held the supply wagons east of the mountains."

Sarah fought another contraction as noon passed. The baby moved constantly now.

"Too soon." Her voice cracked with fear. "James came early too-"

"Different this time." Emma pressed a cool cloth to Sarah's forehead. "We have proper help now. Real shelter."

Margaret arranged her mother's blankets, tucking corners with careful precision. "Angels know about early babies. They helped Mary in the stable."

Caleb watched his children work as Sarah's fever climbed. Emma's medical knowledge had grown beyond her years. Thomas was anticipating needs before they were spoken. Even Margaret helped steadily, carrying water and gathering firewood.

"Your mother survived worse." Midwife Peterson measured more medicine. "Catherine Barrett didn't raise weak daughters."

"Settlement's worried," Thomas reported at dusk. "If more families arrive before supplies-"

"We'll manage." Emma interrupted. "Like we did on the trail."

Sarah's fever broke near midnight. Her skin cooled beneath Caleb's touch as the baby's movement calmed.

"Rest now." Midwife Peterson packed her supplies. "The little one's settled some. Might hold till the proper time."

Thomas took the first watch.

"Pa?" Thomas's voice was soft in the darkness. "Do you think we'll stay here after the baby comes?"

"God willing." Caleb checked Sarah's breathing. "Cooper marked this place for us. Said we'd know when we found a home."

Emma carefully recorded notes in her journal. "We've got enough for a week." She closed the notebook. "If we stretch everything like on the trail."

The night deepened around the cabin as the stars wheeled overhead. They'd settled safely, but survival still demanded careful counting.

Sarah slept quietly now, one hand pressed against where new life grew. The baby had settled some, no longer fighting winter's grip.

13

VALLEY OF PROMISE

Willamette Valley, Oregon Country – Late October, 1843

The first gray light crept over the Willamette Valley as Caleb walked about the frozen ground. His leg burned from the mountain crossing, but dawn revealed what they'd fought three thousand miles to find—rich bottomland stretching toward distant hills, black soil showing through patches of melting snow.

Thomas appeared at his elbow. "Pa. Down there by the creek bend. No claim stakes yet."

Caleb focused his gaze on where Thomas pointed. The boy was right—a perfect homestead site lay unclaimed, with water access and timber in easy reach. Before he could respond, Sarah's sharp gasp cut through the morning air.

"The baby—" Sarah pressed both hands against her belly. "It's time."

Emma moved instantly to support her mother. Caleb caught Sarah's arm as her knees buckled.

"How long?" He kept his voice steady despite the fear tightening his chest.

"Soon." Sarah's fingers dug into his sleeve as another contraction hit. "Very soon."

The valley stretched endless below them—salvation and threat equally balanced. The unclaimed land wouldn't stay empty long. Already, wagon dust marked the horizon where other settlers pushed toward the valley.

"Thomas." Caleb forced his mind to focus. "Take the oxen and our supplies down to that creek bend. Emma, stay with your mother. I'll mark our claim lines."

Thomas was already moving, leading their remaining oxen with sure hands. The animals' ribs showed through winter-thin coats, but they followed the boy's gentle guidance.

"Margaret." Caleb lifted his youngest onto the supply wagon. "Keep the claim stakes dry. We'll need them properly marked."

Sarah fought another contraction as Emma helped her onto her bedroll. The mountain crossing had drained her strength, leaving her pale and shaking.

"The journal." Sarah's voice cracked. "In the medicine chest. Emma knows—"

"I know, Ma," Emma whispered. "Like you taught me."

Caleb grabbed the claim stakes and his father's old axe—five generations of carpentry skills focused now on marking proper corners. The nearest land office representative had to witness their claim, but first, they needed boundaries.

Thomas's voice carried from the creek. "Found something! Old trapper cabin!"

Relief came over Caleb at Thomas' find. Even a broken cabin meant shelter—walls and a roof while Sarah fought through labor.

"Emma!" Sarah's cry cut through his planning. "The baby's coming faster—"

Caleb's leg nearly buckled as he pushed toward the creek. They needed that shelter now.

Margaret's tiny voice rose behind him: "Angels watching, Pa. Like with baby James."

The morning sun cleared the mountains as Caleb reached Thomas at the cabin. The boy had already assessed the structure when he arrived.

"Roof's mostly there." Thomas pointed up. "Some holes, but the beams look solid. Bit of smoke damage inside, but—"

A wagon's rumble cut him off. Through the morning haze, Caleb saw dust approaching from the north—other settlers racing toward the same unclaimed land.

Sarah's next cry carried clearly. The baby wouldn't wait for legal claims or proper shelter. They needed to move now.

"Thomas." Caleb kept his voice steady. "Get your mother inside. I'll mark our corners before that wagon arrives."

The boy didn't hesitate. He was already moving back up the slope.

Caleb drove the first stake deep, marking the northwest corner of their claim. His leg burned with each strike of the axe, but he forced himself through the pain. Five generations of Wheelers had worked wood—now their skills would mark new boundaries.

The approaching wagon grew closer with each passing minute. Caleb could make out four men, all younger than him, all racing toward the same land.

Emma's voice carried from the cabin: "Ma needs you! The baby's coming!"

Caleb drove the second stake. Each boundary had to be proper—straight lines and square corners like his father taught him.

Thomas appeared with their last rope. "Got Ma settled inside. Emma knows what to do, but—"

"Southeast corner next." Caleb passed him the remaining stakes. "Mark it true."

The boy took the stakes and ran. They needed all corners marked before that wagon arrived.

Sarah's cry echoed across their half-marked claim. Caleb's hands shook on the axe handle as he drove the third stake.

The wagon was close enough now to hear voices—young men calling to each other about the perfect bottomland ahead. They hadn't seen the cabin yet and hadn't spotted Thomas marking the far corner.

Caleb's leg buckled as he reached the fourth stakepoint. The mountain crossing had stripped his strength, leaving him running on desperation and fear.

Sarah needed shelter, the baby required walls, and their family needed this land that stretched green and promising below the winter mountains.

The axe rose and fell, marking Wheeler boundaries in Oregon soil—five generations of craft-focused down to this moment—marking home in new territory.

Thomas's voice carried from the southeast corner: "Wagon's turning this way!"

Caleb drove the last stake deep, his father's skills guiding every blow. The boundaries stood true now, marking Wheeler land as clear as any Pennsylvania property line.

Sarah's cry broke through the morning air as the wagon drew closer. Their baby was coming, ready or not.

But they had walls now, boundaries and water, and fertile soil. They had a chance to build something lasting in this valley they'd fought to reach.

Caleb straightened, testing his leg's strength. The pain didn't matter now. They had ground to defend, a child to birth, and a future to build.

The wagon rolled to a stop at their northwest corner. Four young faces studied Caleb's claim stakes with narrow eyes.

Thomas stood beside him now. The morning sun painted their boundaries clear as Sarah fought to bring new life into Oregon soil. They'd crossed half a continent to reach this moment.

The wagon's driver stepped down, hand resting on his rifle. "This land's marked?"

"Wheeler claim." Caleb kept his voice steady. "Proper staked and witnessed."

The wagon men nodded and moved further south in search of their own stake.

Sarah's next cry was solid and sure. Their baby was coming home to a land marked by Wheeler's hands.

The sun climbed higher as morning stretched toward noon. They had boundaries now, shelter, water, and fertile soil—everything they'd dreamed of finding when they left Pennsylvania's familiar land.

A new cry split the air—their baby's first breath in Oregon territory. Caleb stood straight and proud, overcome with emotion.

Sarah's voice carried from the cabin, strong despite her exhaustion: "It's a boy."

Caleb's hands shook as he gripped his father's axe. They were home.

Dawn broke clear and cold across their claim. Caleb woke to find Thomas gone, the door's fresh tracks showing his path to check the animals.

"Bread is baking at the Thompson place," Emma said as she stoked their fire. "Grace said to come for breakfast once Ma's ready."

Sarah sat carefully, cradling James against the winter air that crept through the remaining gaps. The baby's cry softened as he found his breakfast.

"Need to dig a proper cellar." Caleb tested the cabin's floorboards. "Before spring thaw makes mud of everything."

A shout from outside drew his attention. Thomas stood with two boys near his age, all three studying something in the creek.

"Fish weir," Thomas explained when Caleb joined them. "Billy Thompson says we can catch steelhead here when they run."

The Thompson boys had already gathered stones, their hands red and cold as they showed Thomas how to build proper channels.

"Pa says you're a carpenter." Billy stacked another rock. "Could use help with our barn come spring. Trading work, like."

As morning stretched toward noon, more neighbors arrived. Women brought food and birth gifts while men studied the cabin's bones.

"Roof'll need full replacement by summer." Robert Thompson ran his hands over the beams. "Got timber cut if you want to trade work."

"Could use carpentry skills at the mill, too." John Marshall tested a wall. "Pay's fair, and you'd have the first choice of cut lumber."

Sarah received visitors from her bed, James sleeping peacefully between greetings. Each woman brought something useful—dried herbs, spare cloths, and promises of seeds come planting time.

"Community quilting starts next week." Grace Thompson arranged another gift. "It's a Good place to hear what's needed and where."

Margaret sat with the Thompson girls, learning to string dried berries into more elaborate chains.

"For the baby, " the oldest girl pointed to their work. "Ma says new souls need pretty things."

Emma recorded each visitor and gift. Her careful notes would guide their repayments of kindness.

"Like a proper town ledger." Grace nodded approval. "Good to track what's owed in the territory this new."

The land office man returned near noon, and more papers were requiring witnesses.

"Water rights need proper recording." He stamped each document. "Especially with that fish weir the boys are building. Good spot for it - need to mark it legal."

Sarah's voice carried stronger as she signed where indicated.

"Garden space next." The official marked their boundaries on his map. We need to record what's meant for crops versus timber. The territory's particular about agricultural development."

Thomas burst in, winter wind following him through the door. "Pa! Mr. Thompson says we can borrow his plow team come spring!"

"Better mark those field boundaries clear then." The official added another note. "Good bottomland deserves proper working."

More neighbors arrived through the afternoon. John Marshall's wife brought a cradle - rough-made but solid.

"First thing John built when we reached the valley." She touched the smooth wood. "Seems right. It should hold another Oregon baby."

The day settled toward the evening as Caleb rechecked their boundaries. Each stake stood firm despite snow, marking the edges of their new world.

Sarah's voice caught him at the door: "Telling the land good night?"

"Making sure it's real." He settled beside her. "Everything we dreamed of finding."

James stirred against his mother's shoulder, his cry strong.

Emma added wood to their fire while Thomas told Margaret about the fish weir. Their voices mixed with winter wind - family sounds in their walls.

"The garden will go there." Sarah pointed through the door. "Where the sun hits the bottomland first."

"Timber enough for proper buildings too." Caleb shifted to ease his leg. "Once spring makes working easier."

The fire settled, sending shadows dancing across cabin walls. Outside, their claim stakes stood witness beneath winter stars.

14

FIRST LIGHT

Willamette Valley, November, 1843

The first gray light crept over the Willamette Valley as Emma knelt to test the soil. Her fingers pressed into the earth, still damp from yesterday's rain, measuring depth and texture. The garden site stretched before her—thirty paces of rich bottomland caught between the cabin's morning shadow and the creek's gentle curve.

She made another note in her planning journal, recording the spot where wild onions had pushed through overnight frost. Catherine Barrett's careful lists showed which seeds needed the most potent soil, and Emma wouldn't waste an inch of precious ground.

Thomas's voice carried from the property line: "Pa! Found another marker post!"

Sarah appeared in the cabin doorway, baby James cradled against her shoulder. It had been one week since his birth, and already, his cry was more substantial than the winter wind. She swayed gently, humming a lullaby while Margaret arranged pine boughs in the doorway.

"The Henderson place has smoke." Thomas pointed north with his boundary rope. "Think they're accepting morning visitors yet?"

"Let them finish breakfast." Caleb tested the nearest cabin wall, finding gaps that needed chinking before the next storm. "Your mother needs rest more than neighbors need greeting."

Sarah's voice carried from inside: "Emma? Can you fetch more water? The bucket's running low."

"I've got it." Thomas dropped his marking rope and grabbed the water pail. "Emma is busy working in her garden."

Margaret stood in the doorway, her tiny fingers working dried berries into another welcome chain. The settlement children had taught her to string them yesterday, turning Oregon fruit into Pennsylvania-style decorations.

The cabin's walls held steady as Caleb worked, though the roof would need proper attention before spring rains. They'd been lucky to find the trapper's shelter—it had given them four walls and a fireplace while other families still huddled in wagon beds.

A horse's hoofbeats pulled their attention west. Martha Richardson approached atop her bay mare, medical bag strapped behind her saddle.

"Brought more willow bark." The midwife dismounted. "And John Henderson says he's got timber to trade if you're interested."

Sarah appeared in the doorway, adjusting her shawl against the morning chill. "Come in, Martha. The coffee's still hot."

Thomas returned with the water bucket, his face holding excitement in his expression. "I found deer tracks by the creek—fresh ones from this morning."

"Mark their trail," Caleb replied. "We'll need that meat soon enough."

Thunder rolled across distant mountains as morning stretched toward noon. Their first week of homesteading lay behind them, and they had a lifetime of work ahead.

A shout from the north drew their attention. John Henderson rode toward their cabin, his wagon loaded with fresh-cut timber.

"Thought you might need these." The farmer's voice was deep and carried far. "Saw your roof could use some work."

Caleb straightened from his wall inspection. Sometimes survival meant learning which gifts to accept—and how to repay them properly when spring came.

The sun climbed higher as Caleb measured timber with John Henderson.

Martha Richardson's horse stamped impatiently as the midwife checked Sarah's stitches. The cabin's interior had warmed with the morning sun, though gaps in the wall logs still let winter draft whistle through.

"Healing clean." Martha repacked her medical bag. "But you'll need to rest another week at least. No heavy lifting and no long walks."

Sarah adjusted her shawl, one hand pressed against her side. "The garden needs planning before spring. Emma can't do everything alone."

"Emma's doing fine. John Henderson says she's already marked better-growing space than half the settled families." She pulled a small packet from her bag. "Speaking of planning, I brought you some raspberry stars. Good for milk production if you plant them quick."

"Your Thomas has a good eye." Martha watched through the window. "John's boy William could use a friend who knows Eastern ways. Been wild as a winter storm since they lost his mother last spring."

"The Thompson family's hosting dinner tonight." Martha's voice softened. "Sort of welcome feast for new arrivals. You're not right for walking yet, but maybe Emma could bring some of that willow bark tea you're so good at brewing?"

Before Sarah could answer, hoofbeats announced more visitors. Catherine Thompson and her oldest daughter Grace rode up, their saddle bags bulging with covered dishes.

"I brought you some proper food." Catherine's voice was warm as she dismounted. You can't heal right on trail rations and whatever the men shoot."

Grace slid from her horse and moved to help Emma with the garden. The girls formed quick friendships.

"Thomas!" Catherine called. "William's down by the creek. He says he found some good fishing spots if you're interested."

Thomas looked to his father for permission. At Caleb's nod, the boy grabbed his boundary rope and ran to join his new friend.

Martha repacked her medical bag as more neighbors arrived. The Richardson family reached Oregon alone last spring, but the valley's scattered settlers quickly became extended family.

"Rest, " the midwife squeezed Sarah's hand. "The community will help carry you until you're strong again."

The garden site stretched winter-bare as Emma consulted her grandmother's seed lists. Each packet had been carefully preserved during their journey, carrying Pennsylvania wisdom to Oregon soil.

Martha Richardson knelt beside her, checking soil composition with her fingers. "Good earth here. Better than what we found last spring."

Sarah sat in the doorway, James nursing quietly while she sorted through Catherine Barrett's careful notes about medicinal plants. The territory required proof of agricultural development, but a proper herb garden would serve multiple purposes.

"The yarrow should go closer to the cabin." She pointed to Emma's carefully drawn plot. "Where I can reach it easy when the baby's fussing."

Caleb appeared after checking the spring line they discovered yesterday. "Water runs steady here. We can dig an irrigation channel when the spring thaw comes."

Thomas followed with his marking rope, already measuring where the channel should run. The boy had found rich soil deposits during yesterday's timber expedition.

"Deep black earth by the creek bend." He pointed south. "Like the bottom fields back home."

Margaret stood in the middle of Emma's planned plots, carefully planting her first flower—a tiny wild violet she'd found near the spring. "Garden needs pretties, too."

Martha smiled as she checked another soil sample. "She's right about that. Even useful plants grow better with some beauty mixed in."

"Grandmother marked these for late winter planting." Emma showed Martha a seed packet. "But Oregon's seasons run differently."

"They surely do." Martha pointed to where winter wheat still showed green in the Henderson fields. "Spring comes earlier here, but you've got to watch for late frosts."

Caleb and Thomas worked on the irrigation layout, marking where channels would carry spring water to thirsty crops. The boy's skills with rope and measurement proved as applicable in garden planning as timber marking.

"Need to slope it gently." Thomas demonstrated the grade. "Like Mr. Cooper showed us for wagon tracks."

Sarah's voice carried quiet pride as she watched her son work. They'd crossed half a continent watching Thomas grow from child to capable helper. Now, those trail-learned skills have found a new purpose in Oregon soil.

"Willow grows different here." Martha examined Sarah's careful lists. "But the bark works the same. Nature provides what's needed if you know where to look."

15

SEEDS IN NEW SOIL

Wheeler Homestead, Willamette Valley, April 1844

April arrived, bringing clear skies and cool winds across the Willamette Valley. Caleb tested the soil's depth with his father's old dibble stick. Frost still edged the furrows they'd dug yesterday, but the spring sun would warm the earth soon enough.

"Here?" Emma held the first corn kernel ready.

"Deeper." Caleb adjusted her grip on the planting tool. "Soil's richer than Pennsylvania. Seeds need more earth above them."

Sarah appeared from the cabin, baby James bundled against the morning chill. The child had grown strong through the winter months, his cry carrying across the air with a healthy tone.

"Thomas?" Sarah shifted James to check the sun's height. "The beans need dropping before the day warms."

Thomas straightened from where he'd been marking rows with Cooper's old string line. "Just making sure they're straight, Ma. Mr. Cooper said proper rows make weeding easier."

Caleb watched his son measure the garden's boundaries. Each string line ran true as a carpenter's rule.

"The corn goes first." Sarah settled James into his basket near the garden edge. "Five generations of Wheeler planting order."

Emma's fingers moved carefully, dropping seeds into holes her father's stick had made. The first kernel caught morning light as it fell—Catherine Barrett's careful seed saving had given new life to Oregon soil.

"Like Grandmother showed us." Emma's voice carried quiet pride. "Plant with the full moon waning."

Caleb tested another hole's depth. His leg ached less in spring warmth, the damage from the mountain crossing slowly mending.

"Too deep?" Thomas paused in his row marking.

"Just right." Caleb checked the hole's sides. "Oregon Earth knows what it needs."

They worked through early morning, each seed representing another root in the soil. Sarah had arranged their planting carefully, like surgery—corn and beans sharing space.

The settlement's church bell rang across the morning mist, calling children to the newly built schoolhouse. Emma rose from her planting, careful to mark where she'd stopped.

"Best clean up for lessons." Sarah brushed dirt from Emma's skirt. "Take the medical journal - Teacher Matthews wanted to copy the fever remedies."

Emma nodded, already reaching for her grandmother's careful notes. The book had grown thick with pressed plants and added wisdom since Independence.

"I can finish Emma's rows." Thomas grabbed the dibble stick. "Since William and I aren't hunting until afternoon."

Caleb watched Emma disappear toward the schoolhouse, her stern walk matching Sarah's gait. With each passing day, she was becoming more like her mother.

Sarah lifted James from his basket, the baby's morning fussing signaling hunger. "He's growing strong as the corn will."

"Different soil." Caleb kept his tone steady. "Different strength."

They returned to planting as the sun cleared the mountains. Thomas carefully focused on his rows, placing each seed precisely right. Sarah's garden took shape beneath their hands—old knowledge growing new roots in western earth.

The schoolhouse bell rang again, calling lessons to start. But its tone carried promise now instead of parting - Oregon's voice calling their family home.

Thunder rolled across distant peaks as Caleb measured another row. The sound was no longer a threat; spring rains were needed for growing. He planted the next seed deep.

Thomas finished another row, his back straight with pride. "Like this, Pa?"

"Perfect." Caleb checked his son's work. "Cooper taught you well."

The garden would feed them through winter, and Sarah's careful planning ensured survival. However, the garden represented more than food alone. Each seed linked past to future—Pennsylvania wisdom growing new life in their new home.

Emma's steps marked a steady rhythm against the schoolhouse path. Catherine Barrett's journal pressed firm against her slate, its leather binding worn smooth since Independence. Grace Thompson fell in beside her, dark braids swinging with each stride.

"Ma sent dried apples." Grace pulled a cloth-wrapped package from her pocket. "Says your garden planting deserves celebrating."

Mary Henderson joined them at the creek crossing; her new copybook clutched tight. "Teacher Matthews wants us to help with younger children today." Pride lifted her voice. "Says we're ready for proper lessons."

Emma divided Grace's dried apples into careful thirds as they walked. The fruit's sweetness caught the morning sun like a memory—autumn's harvest preserved through winter months.

"Did you bring the fever notes?" Mary's question carried eager hope. "Teacher said we could copy them during lunch."

"Everything Mother wrote about trail cures." Emma patted the journal's worn cover. "Even White Deer's remedies from the desert crossing."

The schoolhouse rose ahead, its fresh-cut timber still sharp against valley green. Other children gathered in the yard—younger ones played marbles while older students compared slate work. The Thompson twins had already started a game of jackstraws, their laughter carrying clear in the morning air.

"Emma!" Teacher Matthews stood in the doorway, his spectacles catching the sun. "Grace, Mary - good. We've got new students needing help with letters."

Inside, fresh-scrubbed benches waited in neat rows. Emma settled at her usual desk, smoothing her skirt like Sarah did before difficult births. The medical journal steadied her hands.

"Show us the pressed flowers first." Grace leaned close as they arranged their slates. "The ones from South Pass."

Emma opened Catherine Barrett's journal carefully as if it were scripture. Dried petals still held mountain colors—purple gentian and yellow columbine preserved between pages of fever cures and birth records.

"Mother says these grow here too." Emma's finger traced dried stems. "Different soil, same medicine."

Teacher Matthews rang the brass bell, its tone sharp and clean across morning voices. Students settled into familiar order—older children helped younger ones while Matthews prepared the day's lessons.

"Emma, " he gestured her forward. "Take the primer group today. Mary, you'll handle numbers. Grace can start copying those medical notes—we'll need them before summer fevers hit."

The younger children gathered around Emma's desk, eyes wide as she opened her slate. She'd learned to shape letters by watching Sarah mix medicines, each mark as precise as measuring fever bark.

"Like this." She demonstrated the letter A, her chalk strokes steady. "Strong lines make clear meaning."

The children bent to their slates, tongues caught between teeth in concentration. Emma moved between desks, adjusting grips and praising effort like Teacher Matthews had shown her.

"Teacher says you're smart as your ma." Little Beth Henderson whispered. "Says you'll be teaching proper soon as you're grown."

Emma kept her voice steady, though pride warmed her chest. "We all learn different ways. Like plants need different soil."

The morning passed in a familiar rhythm—letter practice gave way to sums, then geography lessons spanning half a continent. Emma's careful notes filled fresh pages, knowledge growing sure as garden seeds.

At lunch break, Grace spread their dried apples on clean slate boards. Mary pulled out her copied fever remedies, checking each word against Catherine Barrett's careful script.

"My ma wants the birth chapter next." Mary smoothed the paper carefully, like Sarah with newborn skin. "Proper midwife knowledge will be needed soon as the settlement grows."

Emma divided another apple, sharing the pieces among them. "Mother says knowledge grows best when planted wide."

The afternoon sun slanted golden through schoolhouse windows. Teacher Matthews gathered older students for history lessons while Emma helped younger ones practice letters.

"You've got the gift." Matthews paused beside her desk. "Same as your mother with healing. Different knowledge, same strength."

Emma straightened her slate, pride warming her chest. She'd crossed half a continent watching Sarah tend the sick and injured. Now, she could plant different seeds – knowledge taking root in frontier minds.

Grace and Mary waited by the creek crossing, their friendship steady as mountain streams. Together, they walked the valley path, sharing dreams of teaching between bites of dried apple.

Sarah waited in their cabin doorway, baby James sleeping against her shoulder. "Good lessons?"

"The best." Emma held up her slate. "Teacher says I can help with geography next week."

Thomas Wheeler checked Cooper's old compass, its brass face worn smooth by trail miles. Beside him, William Henderson moved silently like a mountain shadow, their boots leaving no trace in spring mud.

"Track's fresh." William pointed to crushed grass near the creek bend. "Buck passed here before sunrise."

Thomas studied the sign. The deer's hoof marks cut deep—a heavy animal moving slowly in the morning chill. Standing Bear's lessons whispered in his mind: "Patient hunter sees clearest."

"There." Thomas kept his voice low, gesturing toward broken twigs. "Heading for the salt lick we found last week."

William nodded, shifting his rifle with careful grace. The older boy had learned hunting from his father before the trail claimed him. They shared skills like brothers - William's eastern craft mixing with Thomas's trail wisdom.

They moved through fresh-leaved trees, each step careful and deliberate. Thomas had learned stealth watching Pawnee hunters track buffalo.

The salt lick became visible as the morning fog lifted. Deer tracks were everywhere, indicating the animals' regular movements.

"We're close now," William whispered. "Remember what Cooper taught you about wind direction."

Thomas shifted position, putting a breeze against his face. Cooper's voice echoed clear: "Let nature guide your shot. Wind and light work together when you read them right."

Movement flickered at the salt lick's edge. The buck stepped clear of the brush, his rack heavy against the spring sky. Thomas raised his rifle slow and steady, the barrel tracking smoothly.

William held his breath beside him. They'd practiced this shot through winter months, taking more minor games while learning the valley's rhythms. A buck meant meat for both families - proof they'd grown from boys to hunters.

Thomas sighted down Cooper's rifle, measuring distance against windspeed. The buck's shoulder presented a clean target, just as Standing Bear had shown him. His finger found the trigger, pressure steady as mountain streams.

The shot cracked sharp across the morning air. Thomas worked the lever smoothly and surely, watching the buck stagger two steps before falling—his first clean kill since reaching Oregon.

"Perfect." William's voice carried quiet pride. "Right through the heart, like Cooper said."

They approached the fallen deer carefully, as Pawnee taught. The buck lay still, his death clean as Thomas's aim. William pulled his knife, and the handle was worn smoothly.

"You took the shot." William offered the blade. "First cut's yours by right."

Thomas accepted the knife, its weight familiar from trail learning. He'd watched James Davis dress deer through the mountain months, each cut measured against waste and need. Now his hands moved sure as prayer, opening the buck carefully.

"Good blood color." William checked the liver and heart. "Meat's healthy as valley grass."

They worked steadily through the morning heat, and each cut was correctly placed, as Cooper had taught. The meat would feed both families through planting season, Thomas's rifle proving worth equal to Caleb's plow.

William carefully wrapped the organ meat in a clean cloth. "Ma says your mother knows how to cure the liver sweet as sugar."

"My ma learned from White Deer." Thomas separated joints with practiced skill. "Says proper medicine means using everything right."

The sun climbed higher as they dressed their kill. Other settlers' rifles cracked distant across the valley, but Thomas felt pride knowing his shot flew first.

"We should mark this place." William stretched their tired shoulders. "Salt lick draws more deer once summer comes."

Thomas nodded, already planning his next hunt. Standing Bear's wisdom whispered, " A Good hunter thinks three seasons ahead."

They divided the meat fair as trail sharing, each cut wrapped clean in cloth. The morning's work had blooded them proper as men, and frontier skills proved sharp as Eastern learning. The walk home was pleasant through the valley heat. Thomas and William carried their burden proudly.

"Cooper would be proud." William adjusted his pack straps. "Says you read signs better than half the grown men."

Sarah was standing in the cabin doorway when they returned, with one hand shading her eyes.

"Get a clean kill?" She called out.

"Yes, ma'am." Thomas boasted. "Right through the heart"

Caleb tested the barn beam's weight, measuring wood strength against mountain storms. Cooper's design was drawn carefully on tanned leather, spread before him, and each joint was marked for proper fitting.

"Mortise needs more depth." He guided Thomas's chisel grip. "Mountain winds test every weakness."

Thomas worked the tool steadily as Sarah stitched, and the wood chips fell clean and sure. The boy's hands had grown capable through the trail months.

John Henderson appeared through the morning mist, his son William carrying fresh-cut pegs. "Brought oak from that stand we found last week." John tested a peg's grain. "Solid as Pennsylvania timber."

"Proper wood takes proper shaping." Caleb checked Thomas's joint work. "Father always said storms find loose fits first."

They'd worked the barn frame through winter months, each beam cut and shaped between snow storms. Cooper's plan combined eastern building with mountain wisdom—steep roof angles to shed heavy snow and extra bracing against valley winds.

William joined Thomas at the mortising bench; their movements matched from shared labor. "Father says you work wood clean as Cooper promised."

Pride warmed Caleb's chest, though he kept his voice steady. "Good craft needs good teaching. Cooper knew mountain ways better than most."

"Time for the main beam." John Henderson checked the sun's height. "Need all hands before the day heats."

Thomas and William positioned guide ropes while Caleb tested his leg's strength. The injury ached less now, Sarah's medicine and spring warmth bringing slow healing.

"Ready?" Caleb gripped the rope steady. "Lift smooth and sure."

The beam rose like a prayer. Each man knew his task—John guiding from below, boys working the ropes, Caleb monitoring every shift and sway.

The beam settled true in its joints, with marriage marks lining up perfectly. Caleb drove oak pegs home, each strike one step closer to a solid finish.

"Cooper's design holds solid." John tested the joints. "Different wood, same strength."

They worked through morning heat, securing braces Cooper had added for mountain weather. The barn's frame grew closer to completion every hour.

"Like this, Pa?" Thomas positioned a brace. "Angled as Mr. Cooper showed us?"

"Perfect." Caleb checked the fit. "You're reading wood grain true as he taught."

"She'll stand through any storm." John Henderson surveyed their work.

"Time for ridge beam. All hands needed."

They gathered like prayer beneath the morning sun, each man and boy knowing his place. The beam rose smooth and sure. As promised, the ridge beam settled home, and its joints fit clean.

"Good work." John's voice carried quiet pride. "Different timber, same strength."

Thomas and William stood proud as they surveyed the finished barn, their shared labor marking their passage from boys to builders.

Caleb Wheeler stood on their cabin porch as sunset painted the Willamette Valley gold. Their wheat field rippled like water, the spring wind carrying the promise of summer harvest. Sarah appeared beside him, James's baptismal gown held carefully in work-worn hands.

"Found it while organizing the trunk." Her fingers traced the mended tear where mountain crossing had caught the fabric. "Thought it was lost somewhere between South Pass and Snake River."

Caleb watched their planted acres fade into evening shadow. Five generations of Wheeler farming shaped each furrow—skills that carried half a continent, finding new purpose in Oregon soil.

"Remember when Emma wore this?" Sarah smoothed the tiny gown. "Seems like yesterday she was as small as James."

"Different baby." Caleb kept his voice steady. "Different strength."

Their wheat stretched green toward distant mountains, first spring planting taking hold in the valley's rich soil.

"The garden's sprouting." Sarah folded the gown neatly as a prayer. Mother would be proud—her medicines growing strong in Western soil."

"We carried so much." Sarah's voice held more than the baptismal gown's weight. "Lost even more along the way."

"Gained some, too." Caleb touched the gown's worn hem. "Different treasures, same blessing."

James fussed in his cradle as night hunger woke him. Sarah settled in her rocking chair, the baby finding comfort quickly.

Their children's voices carried through the cabin walls—Emma reading to Margaret while Thomas cleaned his rifle. Each sound marked the distance from the Pennsylvania workshop to their new Oregon homestead.

"The wheat's growing strong." Sarah nursed James gently as an evening prayer. "Like your father said it would."

They'd carried the family legacy across the trail—Wheeler carpentry, Barrett healing, and farming knowledge proven through centuries of eastern seasons. Sarah laid the baptismal gown across her lap, its white fabric catching the last mountain light. Between Independence and Oregon, they'd lost so much—tools and treasures, friends and family, certainties traded for survival. But they'd gained other wealth—Thomas's trail craft, Emma's teaching gift, and Margaret's quiet strength. Their children had grown capable as valley wheat, each challenge adding layers of intelligence and maturity.

"We're home." Sarah's voice carried quiet as prayer. "Different land, same hope."

www.ingramcontent.com/pod-product-compliance
Lightning Source LLC
Chambersburg PA
CBHW020133310726
48970CB00006B/1845